Puffin Plus

MARTINI-ON-THE-ROCKS
and other stories

Who ever said school was boring? Certainly no one who's read this entertaining collection of stories! The stars of these stories are ordinary teenagers from ordinary comprehensive schools. But are they really so ordinary? There's fat Kelvin, who's always bottom of the class, until he develops a special talent – for forgery. And the rival love affairs of the two Amandas are anything *but* ordinary! And then there's Leroy, whose artistic talents in a biology textbook got him into trouble in class. And the title story shows that even someone as seemingly insignificant as little Martin can come out tops.

Eight lively, very real and often hilarious stories from a talented author.

D1392213

MARTINI
ON-THE-ROCKS
and other stories

Susan Gregory

Puffin Books

For Kokila, Paul, Greg and gang

Puffin Books, Penguin Books Ltd, Harmondsworth, Middlesex, England
Viking Penguin Inc., 40 West 23rd Street, New York, New York 10010, U.S.A.
Penguin Books Australia Ltd, Ringwood, Victoria, Australia
Penguin Books Canada Ltd, 2801 John Street, Markham, Ontario, Canada L3R 1B4
Penguin Books (N.Z.) Ltd, 182–190 Wairau Road, Auckland 10, New Zealand

First published by Kestrel Books 1984
Published in Puffin Books 1985

Made and printed in Great Britain by
Hazell Watson & Viney Limited,
Member of the BPCC Group,
Aylesbury, Bucks
Set in Bembo

CONTENTS

1
MARTINI-ON-THE-ROCKS

> 'We're the barmy
> Leicester – Rarmy,'

sang the third years of Springfield Secondary. They were travelling by coach for a week's Field Study course in Wales.

'D'ya wanna taste of me steel toe-caps?' shouted John Rogers out of the window at a little lad aged about eight, who stared open-mouthed after the coach. Sir had given John strict instructions *not* to lean out. The others looked on in delight. For one thing John shouted such funny things. For another it would be great when Sir came back up the bus again to sort John out.

'D'ya wanna *die*?' John growled as they passed a short middle-aged man who gaped after the coach looking as if somebody was slowly strangling him from behind. John looked most alarming. He'd just had his hair cut into a skinhead style of a very bristly nature. In fact, he put you in mind of an evil-looking bog brush.

'There's me gran-ma!' he squealed in delight, as they passed the ninety-ninth old lady of the day. 'Don't she walk fast? Last time I saw 'er was twenty minutes ago in Wrexham. *Hiya, Gran!*' he bellowed, as they soared past the tiny figure struggling up the hill. She stopped dead in the middle of the road, staring after the coach, a puzzled expression on her face – and adjusted her hearing aid.

The back seat, who had seen all of this, roared. They were in a holiday mood. They had decorated the back window with their signs:

'Help!! We are being kidnapped.'

'We're of the hairy kind.'

'Cor!'

'Don't follow us. We are lost.'

and

'Keep away! We've got Mr Ridgeway on our bus.'

'Mr Ridgeway. Mr Ridgeway, Sir. Martini feels sick.'

Martin Conway – otherwise known as Martini because he had an Italian mother and because he was very small (teeny, in fact) – tried to smile at Sir but he didn't really feel at all like smiling. Still, he didn't want to upset Sir too much. He knew he was a nuisance, feeling sick.

'Oh, we've got one of those, have we?' said Mr Ridgeway, not sounding too impressed, but coming to the back of the coach nevertheless. '*What* did you want to go sitting on the back seat for, if you're likely to feel sick? Come down to the front where you can get some air.'

Martin nodded feebly and stumbled after Mr Ridgeway down the bus.

'Sit *down*, John,' shouted Mr Ridgeway on his way back, 'and you can get those damn silly notices off the window, all of you, do you hear? *All of them.*'

Martin began to feel a lot better once he was sitting at the front with the window wide open. But he was next to Miss Boothby. He immediately began to feel out of things – and wished he'd kept quiet and not moved. Trust him to land himself sitting by a *teacher* for the journey! Why did he have to be so feeble? Why couldn't he be more like John Rogers?

Someone was humming at the back and they all burst into song:

> ' A little bit of bovver
> And we *all join in!*'

followed by 'WE-ARE-THE-GREATEST', swinging straight back into:

> ' We're the barmy
> Leicester – Rarmy.'

'They *are* barmy. I don't know about anything else,' grumbled Patricia Silcock to Miss Boothby from the seat behind. Martin groaned inwardly. Patricia was the sort of girl who wore sensible shoes. The others called her a creep and they were right! He could just see out of the corner of his eye one of Patricia's sturdy legs finishing in its stout lace-up shoe. How boring! Now if it had been Margaret's leg . . .

Margaret . . . she had to be the most beautiful girl in the third year. He'd signed up for the Wales trip as soon as he'd heard she was going. Trouble was, all the others were after her as well – Danny, Avninder, John. He didn't stand a chance. She'd been laughing fit to burst at John all the way. Martin had a feeling that was partly what had made him feel sick.

At that moment the bus turned another corner and two women of uncertain age came into view, staggering along on improbable heels. It was a country lane and they looked very out of place.

John simply could not resist it. It had to be worth getting into trouble for. He jumped up and leant out again.

''Ullo, darlins,' he bawled. 'Come to me room at the 'ostel, 'alf-past ten, *I'll* show you wot's wot!'

Feeling sick again, Martin could hear Margaret's delighted shriek of laughter over the bellowing of Sir . . .

But half-past ten in the hostel found John, Danny, Avninder and Martin without the company of females. To make up for the sad lack, though, they were also, luckily, without the company of Sir, who was in the dormitory next door with the rest of the party. In their room there were three tanned German boys – students – who were lying in bed reading very earnestly, an American, also a student, who had fascinated them by downing a whole bottle of *milk* (ugh) in his bunk and then fallen promptly asleep, and a much older little man with a weatherbeaten face, a moustache and a very fierce manner who threatened to be nearly as much a pain as Sir would have been. He'd already told them that they were supposed to be quiet at half-past ten and climbed into his bunk, frowning and muttering and looking at his watch. He stared in disapproval at what they were drinking (canned shandy) and told them off for the chewy papers that they were tossing to the floor. This was the life . . .

'Right,' said John, when they were all comfortably settled on their bunks, jaws chomping. 'Anything to report? *I* have!'

'Margaret said she was going to wear her shorts tomorrow if it's sunny. Wha-hoo!' exclaimed Danny, punching upwards with his clenched fist.

'Huh-huh, that's nowt!' said John. 'So we'll see her legs. So what? There's a fire door at the end of that corridor that leads straight into the girls' quarters. It's right by the girls' washrooms. I saw the girls in their knickers 'n' bras. It didn't half make 'em squeal!'

The boys hugged their knees, beside themselves with delight and full of admiration. What a find!

'Did you see Margaret?' asked Martin. He didn't want to seem impressed but he had to know. Trust John!

' 'Course!' said John. 'She isn't half well made.' They all except for Martin burst into explosive giggles.

'*Be quiet*,' said the fierce little man. 'It's well after half-past *ten*. Some of us want to get some *sleep*. It's the hostel *rules*. Rules were made to be kept, not *broken*.'

'Rules were made to be kept, not *broken*,' mimicked

John, but low. The others exploded again. How was it that when you tried not to laugh it always came out much louder?

'Did the girls see you?' whispered back Danny.

' 'Course,' said John again, in a proper voice this time. 'I told you, I made 'em squeal. Oh, and Annette came over to the door to tell me she thinks Margaret wants to go out with me. I think Annette does too, if it comes to that,' said John airily. 'Anyway, then old Boothby caught me. She didn't half yell.'

'I shall be obliged to inform whoever is in charge of you if you don't get into bed properly and *shut up*!' said the fierce little man, sitting bolt upright and revealing his hairy chest.

The boys giggled, exchanging glances, but they clambered into their sheet sleeping-bags and made a show of pulling up their blankets. It wasn't worth the hassle. The fierce man then engaged himself in dispute with the German students about putting the light off. The boys took the opportunity to have another quick conversation.

'Bet I carry Margaret's rucksack for her tomorrow,' said Avninder, not prepared to be put off by John's account of what Annette had said.

'How much?' demanded John. 'You're on.'

'I'll carry more than her rucksack before this week's out, man,' said Danny. 'I'm irre-sis-tible.'

'Who you kidding?' said Avninder. 'And what's that s'posed to mean? "I'll carry more than her rucksack, man." Are you gonna carry *her* up and down the mountains? Just remember, she's well made, like John said.'

'I don't know what you're all getting so excited about,' said John in the darkness. 'She wants to go out with me, I told you, so you all might as well cool it.'

'*Be quiet!*' shouted the little man, beside himself with rage, and you could tell that he was sitting bolt upright again, ready to leap out and yank in Mr Ridgeway. The boys gave in, contenting themselves with flashing their torches around a bit which the little man chose to ignore. Martin flashed his torch with the rest of them but his heart wasn't really in it. He was the only one who truly *cared* about Margaret. He knew he was. How *could* John say those things about her being well made? How ignorant and dirty-minded he was. Still, Margaret was impressed by John, no doubt about that. One thing was certain. It wouldn't be Martin who'd be taking her out by the end of the week. Never in a million years . . .

The next day found the party eating their picnic at the bottom of the fossil rocks. Plenty had happened that morning. Avninder, Danny, Martin and John had had to lay the table for breakfast the night before and Miss Boothby had been furious with them at breakfast because half the cutlery was missing, the rest was skew-whiff and one table had cups but no saucers. Well, it was easy to miss something like that, wasn't it? She went on and on. It was worse than being at home. You could tell that she still hadn't forgiven John for the washroom incident.

After breakfast they'd been allowed an hour to do their own thing in the town while Sir and Miss went for a cup of coffee. The girls all bought Welsh hats and John turned Patricia's inside out and later sat on it. Patricia grew tearful and threatened to tell Miss. 'Aw, don't cry,' John said. 'I'm sorry, honest. It was an accident.' He went up to her and peered into her specs to see if she had stopped crying. He didn't want to be in trouble again for a while. 'Take your specs off, Pat,' he said, sounding quite surprised. Amazed, she did. 'You've got lovely eyes,' he said. 'Come on, you lot. Come and look. Hasn't Pat got lovely eyes?'

She was all smiles in a moment. Martin thought, 'If that was a line, it worked dead well.' The hat was forgotten.

Then Margaret bought a bottle of scent – parma violet. 'I thought I'd treat myself,' she said, and the boys approved – loudly. Loudest of all was John. Then Patricia, who was trying out Margaret's scent, spilt it all over Margaret's rucksack while they were sitting on a slope having a rest on the way to the fossil rocks.

'Pooh! Pooh!' exclaimed all the boys, falling about and holding their noses. All the boys except Martin, that is. He'd watched Margaret's face and she looked as if she was going to cry.

'Thought you were going to carry her rucksack for her, Avninder?' laughed John.

'Pooh, no way,' said Avninder. 'I'm not goin' round smelling like no poofter. You're welcome to your 10p – or whatever it was you bet me.'

Martin would have liked to carry Margaret's rucksack for her, in spite of the smell of parma violets, but he didn't dare ask her. Why couldn't he be cheeky like John? John had demanded to know why she wasn't wearing her shorts that morning – the sun was shining, wasn't it?

Margaret had blushed and tossed her curls. 'Didn't feel like it, did I?' she said.

'You'll feel like it before the week's over,' John had said, winking broadly at Danny. Martin could've kicked his teeth in. Margaret had turned away, scarlet.

Martin looked at John now. He was wearing a flat cap and looked very grown-up and smooth. Danny had his cap on too – it was peaked like John's but with a higher crown.

Why hadn't Martin bothered to buy a cap? It might have made him look older (and taller!).

'Ugh – peanut butter,' said Margaret, opening her sandwich. 'Who'll swap me?'

'I will,' said Martin eagerly, though he hated peanut butter. They swapped sandwiches in silence.

When every chocolate biscuit and can of Coke had disappeared the party divided up into those who wanted to climb to the top of the fossil rocks, those who wanted to stay lower down and hunt for fossils, and those who were too fagged to move at all and were going to stay at the bottom and play cards. Margaret decided she was going to look for fossils. 'Though me trainers are rubbing me!' she complained. Martin cursed himself for not bringing any plasters. Miss told Margaret to go back to the coach to get some.

'I'll go,' offered Martin eagerly. It was just the opportunity he'd been hoping for. He knew Danny, Avninder and John wanted to climb to the top with Sir. He hadn't much of a head for heights and didn't want to go. But at the same time he didn't want to seem yella. If he could arrange it so that he didn't have to go, he would also be able to stay near Margaret . . .

'What a helpful little lad! We'll wait for you then,' mocked John, nudging Avninder. Martin's heart sank. He'd have to go with them. Oh, well.

It turned out to be just as scary climbing as Martin had feared – very steep, and your feet kept slipping from under you. It made Martin feel sick when he looked down; the ground just fell away from you. Far below he could see Margaret bending, hunting for fossils.

Suddenly there was a dreadful clatter above Martin's head and a piece of white rock struck him on the shoulder as he looked up. John had dislodged a bit of the ground and was slipping – in panic he caught hold of an out-jutting sapling and managed to regain his foothold. But he'd displaced a whole lot more rocks and stones which Martin now received full in the face, causing him to lose his footing and his grip. He was falling from quite a height, falling through the air . . .

To Margaret, below him, it was as if it was all in slow motion, then speeding up. Now Martin had hit the ground just above her with a gut-jerking thwack and was still tumbling at a tremendous pace, rolling over and over until his head struck an out-jutting piece of rock and his body crumpled at an unlikely angle.

Margaret thought, 'My God, he's dead!'

He was lying just below her but further along, on a ledge on the steep face of the hillside, and he wasn't moving. Patricia screamed – and broke into hysterical sobs, suddenly clutching at the bristly tufts of grass. Margaret thought, 'Poor, poor Martini! I've got to go to him. Patricia's no use. Oh God, but what shall I do? What shall I do? What if he really is dead?'

She scrambled down and along to him. His eyes were shut.

'Martin, Martin, are you all right?'

What a stupid thing to say! But to her amazement and relief Martin nodded feebly. So he was alive – but how could he possibly know if he was all right?

'Pat, shut up and run and fetch Miss,' shouted Margaret. Then she heard Martin moan and noticed how pale he was. 'What if he does die,' thought Margaret, 'before Miss and Pat get back here? Oh, hurry, hurry.' She realized that she was holding Martin's hand. 'It's all right, Martin. Everything's going to be all right,' she said gently, and Martin nodded, weakly squeezed her hand and opened his eyes for a moment.

By the time Miss arrived at last, carrying the first-aid kit and looking scared, Margaret felt completely in command of the situation. She took the kit from Miss who let it go without a murmur, found the antiseptic and began to bathe the gash on Martin's head. It was bleeding all over the rocks. 'Don't let him be badly hurt,' she prayed inwardly, and as if by a miracle Martin's eyes opened again, this time full of tears.

'It's all right, Martin,' she repeated, and Martin winced, and the silent tears rolled down his cheeks and joined the blood on the rock. 'It's all right, Miss,' Margaret said and somehow she just knew that it would be . . . 'See, the blood's stopping. It's a nasty gash. He'll need stitches – but it's stopping.'

She continued to talk soothingly to Martin while they waited for John to climb and tell Sir who would carry Martin down to the coach. He had moved his head against her knee. She had had to swallow back her own tears when she saw the blood-bespattered rock where his head had lain . . .

It all seemed like a dream to Martin when he was in the doctor's having his head stitched. Well, it wasn't really the doctor's, it was a little cottage hospital. He could remember falling – and the pain – but then it seemed like a blur until he was suddenly aware that his head was resting on Margaret's knee and that she was holding his hand!

'This'll hurt a tiny bit,' said the doctor. Martin nodded absently. What did he care? *He'd had his head on Margaret's knee!* Of course, it meant – nothing – nothing at all – but she'd looked after him, and he'd remember it all his life. How wonderful she was!

When he came out he had a magnificent bandage round his head but his hair was still all matted with blood. 'No signs of concussion, luckily,' said the doctor to Sir and Miss. The others all cheered loudly when they saw him but Margaret went straight up to him. 'You were so brave, Martin,' she said. 'Your poor head! When we get back to the hostel I'll wash away all that blood for you.'

Danny, Avninder and most of all John just stood and stared!

Margaret hummed as she gently lathered Martin's hair, taking great care not to wet the blood-soaked wad of lint that covered the stitches. She told Martin she wanted to be a doctor when she grew up. She chatted on. Martin kept getting stuck for words.

'I know you must have hated it when you hurt yourself,' she said, 'and when you had to have the stitches, but what do you think of it all so far?'

'It's better than school,' said Martin cautiously. Then he threw caution to the winds, and decided to live dangerously. 'It's great.' Inspiration seized him. 'What do *you* think?'

'Oh, it's all right,' she said. 'Yeah, not bad at all really. Only thing is – I know I shouldn't say this because they're mates of yours – but Danny and John and Avninder are beginning to get on my nerves. They're dead childish, aren't they? Specially John. He's such a big-head. And those stupid caps they wear. They think they're It, don't they? And they're really embarrassing. All they ever think about is sex. You're not very like them really, are you?'

Martin hastily agreed with her that he was *not*! He resolved to keep his thoughts about her absolutely clean from now on. But it was very difficult. They were in the games-room now – and she was leaning all over him, blowing his hair dry and gently pushing her fingers through it! John and the gang were pretending to play table football – but they kept turning round to stare in blank astonishment. Martin also noticed to his surprise that Patricia had taken off her specs! And her sensible shoes! And her socks! And she was painting her toenails with Margaret's nail varnish. She kept looking up and blinking in the direction of John!

In the dormitory that night the fierce-looking man had a much better time of it. The gang were very quiet, stunned by the way that Margaret had fussed over Martini. Avninder even said to Martin, 'How do you do it, mate?' and Martin said casually, 'Oh, it's just a knack.'

John said, 'Of course, it's only because you hurt your head. There's nothing in it,' but he didn't sound too sure, and the others looked very doubtful.

They were worn out after all the climbing and the fresh air. They flashed their torches for a little while just to keep up appearances, but they were soon asleep.

All except Martin. He was definitely in love, he decided. But she only thought of him as a friend, like John said, didn't she? She didn't want it to be anything more. And she didn't like John's dirty talk. Come to think of it, *she didn't like John*! So why not have a go? He couldn't just be friends with her, not now. Not now he'd felt her fingers in his hair. He must have courage. He had to be bold. Yes, it was definitely worth a try. The worst thing that could happen was that she wouldn't speak to him any more. But he'd still be able to see her . . .

The next day dawned bright and sunny. Martin climbed out of his bunk bed filled with determination. As soon as he came into the dining-room Margaret waved at him.

'How's your head?' she shouted cheerily. And she'd saved him a place!

After breakfast in the yard in front of the boot-room Martin said casually, 'Here, Margaret, I'll carry your rucksack.' She blushed and looked pleased. Carrying it as well as his own, Martin felt like a giant. He could do anything he set out to do today.

Climbing the hill at the back of the hostel behind Margaret he decided that the moment had come. He quickened his pace and caught up with her. He'd been rehearsing this in bed all last night. 'Beautiful from up here, ain't it?' he said, and casually put his arm round her as they paused to admire the view, waiting for all hell to be let loose.

But this didn't happen! In fact, Margaret very quickly put her arm around him! This was a bit difficult on account of the two rucksacks. They continued up the hill like that. It made climbing extremely heavy going. They laboured on in the sunshine, perfectly happy.

John from just behind them simply couldn't believe his eyes. That midget Martini with his baby face! Margaret was a whole head taller than he was! She couldn't really have fallen for him, could she? No, it was because of his tumble. Yes, she was mothering him, that's what it was. Well, he'd soon put a stop to that. The likes of Margaret needed a man, not a boy!

He caught them up. Unfortunately he was panting more than he'd liked to have been.

'Thirsty work – all this climbing,' he said, taking off his cap and wiping his forehead. 'Bet you could use a drink, Maggie. I'll treat you when we get to a pub. What'll it be?'

Margaret thought for a minute while Martin's heart sank to the bottom of his climbing boots. Here it had to end.

This would show Margaret that John wasn't really childish – suggesting they should go to a pub, all casual like that, and when they were with the teachers as well!

But Margaret was staring at John as though she'd just smelt something nasty. 'Oh, I think I'll have a Martini-on-the-Rocks, thank you, John,' she said at last. 'That makes such a nice *change*. In fact, I'd really *like* one of those.'

2
S.H.C.

When Mrs Hopkins left to have a baby, One Set Two had a new teacher for English. The new teacher was soft and did a lot of grinning. You could tell her *anything*. They called her Smiler. She smiled on and on, even when they made a racket. One Set Two thought she wasn't quite right in the head.

On this particular morning, the boys came charging into Smiler's room before the girls, hot-foot from Registration. Some pulled up abruptly as they crashed across the threshold, as if an invisible rider had yanked hard on an imaginary rein. They looked across at Smiler. But she never said, 'Go out and form a line and do it *properly* this time.' She just smiled on.

'Miss, Miss!' yelled Gary Radford, flapping the air with *Adventures in Science*, Issue One. He was building it up into an encyclopedia. 'Will you read us a bit out of this? It's dead good – all about S.H.C.'

'S.H.C.?' smiled Smiler, raising an eyebrow and scratching her nose. 'What's S.H.C.?'

'Spontaneous Human Combustion. It says this man went up in flames when he was just sitting on the *bog*. It says it's caused by stress.'

The girls, who didn't charge through the door but appeared to sleepwalk in, leaning at an angle of forty-five degrees to the door jambs and one another, groaned heavily. 'Aw, Miss. Don't let them get on to S.H.C. It takes for ever.'

Three others had joined Gary, clamouring round Miss at the table, jabbing well-chewed fingers at the pictures. 'Look at *this*, Miss. Isn't it 'orrible?' 'Go on, read it, Miss.' 'Yeah, Miss! I've got this book all about S.H.C. at home, Miss. I'll bring it in tomorrer.'

'Mrs Walker!' A tall thin figure at the door. All eyes swivelled to it. The Deputy Headmistress, quivering like a compass needle.

'I don't think One Set Two has time to waste being read to, Mrs Walker. One Set Two cannot spell "cuneiform". They cannot spell "Tutankhamun". One Set Two cannot even spell "pyramid" or "papyrus".' Flecks of spit flew before Mrs Cuthbert's words and she scanned the class, like a ship's beam, for gigglers. 'I thought, Mrs Walker, that you might outline the story of Antony and Cleopatra for them this morning. To assist them with their History. I am all in favour, One Set Two, of an integrated curriculum.' And with that she cruised off.

One Set Two looked a little stunned. 'She's all in favour of a what-er?' asked Barbara Heyward.

'Summat to do with curry, weren't it?' said David Wheeler. 'Must be a Paki-lover.'

'Shurrup, you,' growled Baljit Singh, shoving David.

'Shurrup, yourself, Sing-a-Song-of-Sixpence,' said David, snatching Baljit's rubber and flicking it across to Peter Kilbourne who fielded it neatly.

'Mrs Cuthbert dictates History that fast,' grumbled Sharon Perkins, 'me arm feels like it's gonna drop off.'

'Well now,' said Mrs Walker, hitching her skirt and sitting on the edge of the table. 'Antony and Cleopatra. Cleopatra was an adventurous lady. She was once delivered to a man rolled up in a carpet.'

One Set Two punched one another in delight and giggled and whispered behind their hands and settled down.

'Can we act it, Miss?' said Julie Hill who fancied being Cleopatra.

'Yeah,' said David Wheeler, turning his head till his nose was parallel with his shoulder and talking out of the side of his mouth. 'And you can be the carpet, baby.'

'Cleopatra put an asp to her busom,' wrote Gary Radford that evening in the exercise book he used for a diary. 'An asp is a venomous serpent. She must've got *sucked* to death.' Gary looked thoughtfully at what he'd just written. This week he was practising writing very, very small. He was currently averaging twenty-two words to the line. The Deputy Head had written, 'This is the work of a demented ant', in big letters across his History book. He looked back at last week's entries. Last week he'd been into topping his 'i's and 'j's with little circles instead of dots, and the Deputy Head had written, 'Stop this affectation', and the week before that he'd done great looping 'g's and 'y's, heavy as pears, drooping on to the line below. He didn't have room for the words and had to squash them all up and even he'd got confused. The Deputy Head had written, 'Contracted the dropsy?' He didn't know what she was on about in any of them.

Gary turned his thoughts away from his handwriting and back to Cleopatra. How horrible to be sucked to death by a snake! No more horrible, though, than spontaneously to combust. Gary shifted in his chair and began to tear at the skin round his fingers with his teeth. Was there some warning when it was going to happen? Could you feel yourself hotting up? They say it's caused by stress. Gary was under a lot of stress at the moment. Apart from worrying that he might burst into flames at any moment, he was worried that Mrs Walker might not be teaching him English properly. His mam was dead set on him getting O-levels like his cousin Ian. Only another five years and he'd be taking them. He was also worried because everybody in his class had suddenly started fancying everybody else and all he wanted in life was a ferret. He felt very alone. He put a hand to his forehead. Pretty hot. He turned out the electric fire in his bedroom and went across to the bathroom to splash cold water on his face. That should cool him down. He pushed a lot of bottles and packets

around in the bathroom cupboard looking for a thermo-
meter. If his temperature was up, he'd take a cold bath . . .

When the boys came tearing into Mrs Walker's room
the next day they showed her 'The Beckoning Lady' in
Adventures in Science. It came under the section 'Appari-
tions, Poltergeists and E.S.P.' and told how a woman
woke one night to see a ghost dressed in grey with an
old-fashioned bonnet walk out of her wardrobe and stand
by her bed. The ghost didn't *do* anything – just looked
down on the woman without smiling. The same thing
happened the next night. But the night after that the
grey lady crossed to the window and beckoned. 'And I
knew then,' said the woman, 'that what she wanted was
to entice me to jump to my death.' She had every reason
to think so, too, living on the thirty-third floor of a
high-rise block. The girls, who loped into the room in
the middle of Mrs Walker reading the story, shuddered
and clutched each other. All except Julie Hill who was
stuck in the doorway between a suitcase and what looked
like a large roll of carpet.

'I had this dream once,' said Gary in a low voice to Mrs
Walker as she waved the rest of the class to their places,
'that I was looking at my own tombstone.' He said it low
because in point of fact he'd seen it on 'Strange Tales' on
the telly. He didn't suppose Mrs Walker ever watched
'Strange Tales'. All teachers watch is the Last Night of the
Proms and Party Political Broadcasts.

'Tutankhamun,' said Mrs Walker when at last they had
settled down and were still, 'was a king and he died very
young.' Gary began to feel himself hotting up. 'He married
a child bride.' Gary felt himself getting yet hotter. 'The
two of them were not much older than you lot. When he
died he was only in his teens and they buried him in the

Valley of the Kings. In a tomb of gold within a room of gold, with a gold chariot, and a death mask of gold upon his face. Can you imagine what it was like when they found the entrance to the tomb, only this century, and room after golden room?' One Set Two stirred. 'On top of his tomb,' said Mrs Walker, 'his bride placed a garland of flowers. Think how sad she must have been. The tomb was sealed up and the air was so still that the flowers remained intact for over three thousand years. But when they opened up the chamber, the air got in and the flowers just crumbled into dust.' One Set Two sighed and were still.

'Can we do Cleopatra now, Miss?' asked Julie Hill at last. 'I've brought a bit of carpet in, Miss,' and she yanked up the roll from the gangway to show Mrs Walker.

'All right,' said Mrs Walker, 'but just let's go over the story once again. If you remember, Antony was Cleopatra's boy-friend much later than the carpet incident. Who was Cleopatra's boy-friend earlier on, when she was delivered all rolled up?'

Gary's hand shot up. A look of intense pain came over his face, as he gripped his armpit with his other hand and flicked from the wrist as if he wanted shut of his fingers for ever. 'Miss. Oooh, Miss.'

'Yes, Gary.'

'Caesar, Miss,' said Gary crisply, looking triumphantly round at the others as if expecting a standing ovation. Julie Hill pulled her eyes down at the corners at him till the reds showed.

'Quite right, Gary,' said Mrs Walker, 'and since you show such enthusiasm, I think you should play the part of Caesar, don't you?'

The class cheered and Gary buckled up. '*Oh, no*, Miss. Please.' Julie Hill squealed in distress, rolled down her lower lip and dashed her face into her hands, but very soon recovered. 'I've brought a costume as well, Miss,' she said, now hoisting up the suitcase. 'Can I go to the toilets to change?'

Mrs Walker gave permission and Julie, hardly able to believe her luck, said quickly, 'Can Sharon come too, Miss, to help me get ready?' She stuck up both thumbs and nodded her head very fast at her friend like a chicken pecking corn. The two of them dashed out, leaving the class to dream up suitable clothing for Imperial Caesar.

Fifteen minutes later Julie and Sharon returned, bent double with laughing, holding one another up. Cleopatra wore her coat clutched round her middle like a dressing-gown and from underneath floated a lot of shocking pink net. Her eyes had been alarmingly extended towards her eyebrows with bat wings of blue paint and edged with wiggly black lines. Her lips were plastered thick as raspberry jam on toast. She wore a gold head-band slung low across her brow from which sprouted a peacock feather so long it bent as she entered the door. Across her forehead, cheeks and chin she had stuck pink and purple sequins and she jangled at the wrist and ankle with lines and lines of bracelets, and row upon row of beads clinked against the studs of what looked like a dog-collar round her neck. She waded into the room on four-inch stiletto mules.

Four handmaidens and four carpet-bearers were sent off to wrap up the human parcel and at last the carpet was carried shoulder high from the jumping horse just outside the door with Julie Hill ceremonially rolled up inside it. Or, rather, her head and body were rolled up but her legs stuck out at the other end like a mummified clothes-peg. With a jerk and a bump the package was placed on the ground at the feet of Imperial Caesar who wore five tea towels borrowed from the Home Economics block for a toga. Two round his legs, two round his body and one draped becomingly over one shoulder. On his head he wore a crown of wire with a few browning ivy leaves growing out of it. Baljit Singh, who was the carpet-seller, said, 'I have a fine piece from the East for your delight, O Caesar,' and with a flourish unrolled the carpet with his foot. Up jumped Julie Hill, hair and eyes wild, cheeks red as crab-apples, and Caesar the Great choked and clutched himself with horror as a great wave of blistering heat broke over him at the sight of her, and the Deputy Head walked in.

What the Deputy Head saw was One Set Two jumping up and down in the gangways, One Set Two kneeling on desks, One Set Two gasping for breath and clinging on to one another and generally falling about. That terrible Julie Hill was leaping up like a Hollywood star out of a birthday cake, wearing what looked like her mother's négligée and an awful lot of jewellery and little else besides. And Gary Radford was dressed entirely in tea towels with *ivy leaves* in his hair and was clearly over-excited.

'*Mrs Walker!*' bellowed the Deputy Head. All eyes rushed to her, iron filings to a magnet. 'Can I have a word with you, please, *outside*.' Gary completely forgot that he was about to combust spontaneously in the delighted realization that if anybody was going to, it would be the Deputy Head. She was as blotchy as salami and turning purple fast.

But when the Deputy Head returned five minutes later there was no sign of scorch marks, worse luck. She rapidly put an end to five glorious minutes during which One Set Two had run entirely amok. Cleopatra had married Caesar under a deluge of English exercise-book confetti and the happy couple were still sparkle-eyed and clutching hands. Four more girls had laid claim to four more boys by leaping out at them from a series of carpet packages and there was just about to be a mass wedding and another great confetti storm when the Deputy Head walked in for the second time.

Slowly, very slowly, like those suffering from hangovers after the most tremendous night on the town, One Set Two gathered up every scrap of confetti. The Deputy Head yanked Julie off to the cloakroom and personally supervised, arms crossed, while she scrubbed off every bit of the bat wings and the raspberry jam. Then she confiscated the magic carpet. 'Mrs Walker will no longer be taking you for English, One Set Two,' concluded the Deputy Head. 'I shall take that little responsibility entirely upon my own shoulders and from now on this period on a Friday will be given up entirely to a *Spelling Test*!'

But Gary hardly heard. Since he hadn't spontaneously combusted, that searing blast of heat could mean only one thing. *He actually fancied Julie Hill and he wasn't a freak after all*. And she'd married him in the face of Mrs Walker and an entire congregation.

Julie and Gary sat on the wall by the bus stop after school with their arms round one another. Gary didn't remove his arm even when Mrs Walker grinned into view. He looked at her curiously instead for any signs of albino rabbit pink eyes but she didn't look in the slightest put out. In fact she just carried straight on grinning. 'Have a good week-end, both of you,' she said, 'and don't go up in smoke.'

Gary grinned politely at her. 'No, we won't,' he said, and pulled Julie off the wall, keeping hold of her hand and whistling, as the bus came. No danger of that any longer, now he felt so grown-up and cool. He wasn't under any stress now, either, since they wouldn't be having Smiler for English. He was really glad about that. What with having the Deputy Head for Spelling every Friday, a whole galaxy of O-levels was positively guaranteed. He'd show his mam. He'd do just as good at school as his cousin Ian. And no sweat.

3
MERIT MARKS

'A merit mark a day,' said Mr Warner, 'keeps Two Trafalgar away.'

Two Trafalgar were Two Bosworth's keenest rivals for the Achievement Cup. Kelvin Grant took a bitter look at the merit mark chart that Mr Warner was now drawing Two Bosworth's attention to. He only rated the thinnest green line just scratching the very bottom of his column on the graph. He looked glumly at the great mountain peaks scaled effortlessly by the likes of Penny Weston and Raju Mistry, which Mr Warner was even now pointing to with the end of a ruler. He didn't even smile when Trevor Langston let out a long sigh, rolled his eyes and whispered for all to hear, 'I don't know how you do it, Raju. It's a Mistry to me,' though the rest of the class released a howl and even Mr Warner quivered. But Mr Warner recovered fast enough to remember to point out Kelvin's graze mark as the most disgusting sight in the whole history of Two Bosworth. 'Pity modern technology hasn't come up with brain transplants yet,' said Mr Warner. The class laughed and turned to stare. Kelvin kept his head well down, pulling his eyebrows tight together as curtains, while he added Mr Warner to his Death List and coloured him in a four-star rating. On the Death List already were the Senior Mistress, the Headmaster, the lollipop lady and the whole of Two Bosworth. Two Bosworth being, of course, the year and the House to which Kelvin belonged. And he hadn't a friend in either.

The Death List was contained in a small hard-backed black notebook with 'Kelvin's Death List' written on the front page, coloured red, with blood dripping from it. The front page also had a bell, book and candle in one corner, a skull and crossbones in another, well-used fangs and a very small garlic clove in a third, and in the fourth a

35

skeleton with a military moustache raising on high a cane
as thick as a truncheon – Mr Wheelwright, the Headmaster.
Kelvin liked to draw. He could get it right when he drew.
It was when he wrote it down that it kept coming out
incredibly wrong. Even he could see that afterwards when
he compared his way of looking at words with the way
everybody else seemed to do it. The first page of the
notebook would read to anybody else as 'Klevisn Daeht
Lsit'. And who could get merit marks for that?

'Right-oh, Two Bosworth,' said Mr Warner, spinning
round from adding another five strata to Raju Mistry's
mountain. (Raju Mistry averaged at least two merit marks
a day, so what did it matter about Kelvin anyway?) 'Line
up for Assembly, boys first. *Line* up, Lee Simmonds. Don't
rev up. And no racket on the way in. We don't want to be
straight back to do it again.'

The Senior Mistress was supervising seating this morning. 'I want you to sit, School,' she said grandly, 'as a *body*.'
She spread her arms to show the unity of movement she
had in mind. School couldn't seem to get it right at all.
Soon they were bobbing up and down like maroon and
golden yo-yos. Kelvin, when his backside at last found a
haven, discovered he had laid it to rest on Penny Weston's
cardigan sleeve. (All the exercise had made her very warm
and she'd curled her cardi neat as a cat in the gap between
the boys' line and the girls'.) The problem was that Kelvin's
backside spread so much that he needed a space and a half
to be settled in comfort. Penny's lip rose to her nose in
disgust. 'Get your bum off, Dumbo,' she hissed, snatching
at her garment and tugging. Kelvin's ample fingers caressed
the Death List in his blazer pocket. They had to sing the
first verse of 'Jesus bids us shine' four times. 'I *had* meant
to talk about being brave, obedient and persevering,'

snarled the Headmaster. 'But some of you can't even hold your heads up.'

On the way to first lesson Kelvin heard Trevor Langston and Terry Griffith talking about him.

'You don't like 'im then.'

'I hate 'im.'

'Why do you hate 'im?'

'Because he never goes out and he doesn't wear a Parka.'

And even though Kelvin passed the Art master in the corridor and he shot up his eyebrows and wiggled his beard, the nearest Mr Keane ever came to showing he approved of a kid, Kelvin didn't smile.

Miss Irving was in one of her bouncing moods (very unrestful). As soon as Two Bosworth sat down, three chairs gave way. Chairs were always giving way in Miss Irving's lessons. She was new to the school that term and, like a see-saw, newest teacher meant oldest chairs. Mr Nowall, the caretaker, didn't like Miss Irving. 'Careful with them chairs now, Miss Irving,' he always said as she lined her classes up to go into Room Six. 'I don't know what your classes get up to with them, I reely don't.' You could tell he meant karate practice at least. In fact, Miss Irving's classes were very orderly. They had to pick up every scrap of paper that had dropped to the floor before leaving and nudge the desks back into perfectly straight lines. The cleaning lady loved Miss Irving and was going to give her a Busy Lizzie for Christmas.

After the caretaker had had his usual words with Miss Irving outside the door this morning, she had turned redder than ever and everything had bounced around a good deal on the way in.

'Please, Miss, this chair's wobbly too,' whined Hazel Bishop as soon as the first three chairs of the day had given way. She shuffled her bottom backwards and forwards to demonstrate. 'Mine squeaks,' said Trevor Langston, making it whimper like a stamped-on puppy. 'Mine's got a broken-off bar.' Penny Weston twizzled it on high like a drum majorette. 'Mees, Mees, I 'ave *poosh* my brokinoff bar into the *'ole*, Mees. Can I 'ave a merry mark?'

Miss Irving managed to stop herself mid-bounce. 'This morning,' she said, almost without moving her lips – Kelvin was impressed, 'this morning we are going to *count* the number of chairs that are on their last legs. Then we shall inform the caretaker. Then we shall see what he is prepared to do about it.' Two Bosworth thought this was a grand idea. Well, at any rate, better than Maths. 'Miss, Miss, mine is, Miss.' '*Definitely*, Miss.' 'Look at *this*, Miss. This is *unsafe*.' Penny Weston proved her point by wriggling and the chair exploded beneath her. She got up from the floor, smile gone, rubbing hard at her back. Miss Irving bounced around her in concern.

Kelvin was much taken by Penny Weston's manoeuvre. When Miss Irving had her back to Kelvin he lifted his bottom a few inches off his chair and let it drop. The chair went off like a car backfiring. Kelvin felt power race through him like a current, making the layers and layers of spare flesh spark into life. The class shot to their feet with the force of their laughter. Somebody clapped him on his back. Kelvin smiled a fat smile. This was better than Death Lists.

Miss Irving eyed him grimly. Then she went to the front and tore a piece of paper from a notebook and made wild dashes at it with a pen. She folded it and held it up and out. 'You can take this note, Kelvin, to Mr Nowall, informing him that five chairs are in pieces and a further twenty-three on the verge of collapse, and asking what he suggests.'

By the time Kelvin returned he had decided that the days of the Death List were by no means over. "E's off to see the 'Ead, Miss,' he informed her with an air of deep gloom. "E says 'e's going to get union advice but likely 'e'll be takin' industrial action. Strike, Miss,' added Kelvin dolefully, 'on account you've accused 'im of not doin' 'is job proper.' Kelvin's mind was not really on the news he was passing on to Miss Irving but on the remarks addressed to him by the caretaker. They were along the lines of a direct link-up between Kelvin and the mass destruction of the woodwork in Room Six, and size had figured largely in the accusation.

When Two Bosworth went back to their own room for Geography it was to discover that Mr Pritchard was away. They'd got The Mouse instead. Kelvin cheered up a little. The Mouse taught Needlework to the lower school. She whispered and she lisped. She twitched her nose. She had soft dark hairs along her upper lip like the downiest of whiskers. This morning The Mouse spent a long time tugging at cupboard doors without getting anywhere and at last decided that they must be locked. She sent Kelvin (who always sat at the nearest point to any escape route in case of earthquake, fire or flood) for the key. Kelvin remembered the joy of carrying the whole class with him when his chair went off, and dropped the key into a rather perished looking rubber plant on his way back to the classroom.

'Wasn't there, Miss,' he said, heaving his fat shoulders as he came through the door. "E must've took it 'ome with 'im. We can't 'ave no Geography.' The class cheered and someone threw up a book. Kelvin felt that tingle again and added quickly, 'I could go to the Art Room and get some paper and paints, Miss. We could do, like, you know, projects.' 'Yeah, yeah!' clamoured Two Bosworth and a few banged their desk lids to underline their approval. The Mouse darted a glance in the direction of the wooden partition. It was all that separated her from Mr Ross (Geology, a tartar) and she twitched all over. 'Very well then,' she mouthed in their direction. 'But if I let you, you mutht promith not to make any noithe whatthoever.' 'We promith,' bellowed Two Bosworth cheerily and another four desk lids clattered as back-up.

'We could make Christmas cards, Miss,' said Penny Weston. It was the beginning of October. 'You can never start getting ready too early, my mum always says. Bring some glitter and some glue, Kelvin.' She turned on him a smile that nearly cancelled out the cardigan sleeve. Ten minutes and much banging of desk lids later, Kelvin staggered back, hardly anything showing behind glue pots, giant rolls of paper, paint pots and card. He looked like Playaway Educational on legs. The class gave loud lisp to their appreciation. There was a rapping on the partition behind which the fifth year pursued their O-levels, one frantic poltergeist among a multitude of very silent dead.

Two Bosworth settled to their labours. Penny Weston had soon opened a whole production line of card-makers. She kept sending Raju Mistry to the medical room for more cotton wool. 'You can be Product Manager,' she bribed him. 'But I shall be Managing Director.'

Kelvin set up a collapsible stable in rivalry and very soon most of the boys were copying the prototype. Trevor Langston and Terry Griffith dropped the glue brush in the glue and went in for a lot of sticky fishing. Penny Weston came to the rescue by inserting two pencils after the manner of chopsticks and levering it out. The noise level was high and The Mouse quivery. Kelvin worked on, remembering the throb and tingle of having the whole class behind him. Ideas were ballooning around in his head.

When the bell rang for Break the girls (not Penny Weston) offered to clear up the mess for The Mouse. She let them, not like Miss Irving who would have made the boys do it because girls weren't put on this earth to be slaves.

At Registration next morning Mr Warner had bad news for them. 'Two Trafalgar are well in the lead, Two Bosworth,' he said. 'What have you been playing at?' Kelvin shuddered. In a moment there'd be another merit mark tally and he'd be found wanting. An idea from yesterday slowly rose like a bubble in his mind. His nylon shirt stuck fast. His felt tip slid slimily from his hand.

He would become a manufacturer of merit marks. He would turn himself into Kelvin's Magnificent Merit Mark Factory. Not in his own name, of course. He'd forge merit marks on behalf of the cleverest kids in the class . . .

But how would he get hold of the slips in the first place?

The chance came in the very next lesson. The Geography master was still away but today they had the Senior Mistress, not The Mouse. She gave them mental arithmetic and Raju Mistry got full marks. 'Very well done *indeed*, Mistry,' she said, and Raju said modestly, 'Well, I must admit I was lucky with some of my guesses.' 'Who'll fetch me some merit mark slips?' asked the Senior Mistress. Kelvin, who had now taken to sitting at the very front and as near the teacher as possible, the better to control what was going on, shot up his arm. He also rose seventeen inches from his seat and swayed, so blocking out all opposition. The Senior Mistress looked on him with distaste. 'Granted, Grant,' she said at last, her frown changing to a whinnying leer.

Luckily it was The Mouse who opened the staff-room door and not, say, Mr Ross, who counted out merit mark slips like a miser counts out gold. She passed over a great mound in her anxiety that Kelvin should be gone. The staff-room was The Mouse's hole. It would have to be a very tasty cheese indeed to tempt her out in the face of all those cats.

Kelvin launched the merit mark drive over Break. He locked himself in the bogs and forged away like a very round gnome. 'Gi'us a look at your merit marks,' he'd said to Raju. With great care, behind the barrage balloon of his arm, he'd taken down the details, checking the letters backwards and forwards and backwards and forwards so as not to get them all mixed up. Name: Raju Mistry. Number of Merit Marks: (No more than three allowed for any one piece of work). House: Two Bosworth. Initials of member of staff. Then he took notes from Penny Weston's slips. Finally he posted the first newly minted batch into the yellow box in the hall, marked Bosworth House.

After the next merit mark count, Mr Warner came in like the rising sun. 'Bosworth well in the lead. Trafalgar truly trounced. Atcha, Two Bosworth!' He made a clenched fist. 'We'll show 'em.' Kelvin felt the now familiar throb and glow. Pity nobody would ever know how he'd done his bit. But such is life.

Whenever Kelvin needed merit mark slips, he sought out The Mouse. He waylaid her on the stairs; he blocked her getaway when she scuttled for staff toilets; he haunted her new hidey-hole, the lab. assistant's prep. room, where the lab. assistant and The Mouse would smoke and quiver and smoke and dart little frightened eyes towards the door. To The Mouse it seemed that forever now the monstrous shadow of Kelvin Grant must fall fatly across her path. She would turn pale as soon as she saw Kelvin heaving into view and dive for cover. But in vain, for she knew there was one thing and one thing only that would satisfy the beast, and at last she would emerge, clutching great fistfuls of merit mark slips. These she would thrust gratefully into Kelvin's hand like ransom money, thanking him over and over. Anything, anything at all, if only the fat fiend would just let her be for another three, four, five days. For the first time in Mount Olive Secondary, a worm had turned. The Mouse became The Mole.

The Great Bosworth Success Story continued up to Christmas. By that time Kelvin had got the business of saving Bosworth House down to a fine art. He didn't allow power to go to his head – no extremes. He was afraid that if life became too desperate for Trafalgar some bright spark might come up with the same idea. Then the bottom would fall out of the merit mark market, and they'd be trundling merit mark slips off in barrel loads, like what happened to the German mark in the twenties.

After the Carol Concert Kelvin decided that he would slip a last couple of merit marks into Bosworth's yellow box on behalf of Raju Mistry and Penny Weston. Just for good luck. Kelvin's hand slid towards the box as he went back to the classroom. In went the slip with Raju Mistry's name on it and he was just about to post Penny Weston's when he felt a hand clamp his shoulder and he twirled round in horror to look straight into the eyes of . . .

Penny Weston herself!

Kelvin let go of the merit mark slip in his panic and Penny Weston snatched at it as it fell, as you might snatch at a moth. 'You're always posting merit marks these days,' she said without opening her hand, giving him a slantwise look. 'How come *you* win so many?' She unravelled the screwed-up slip and gasped. 'It's *mine*, you creep! What you been stealing my merit marks for?' Then she looked at it more closely. 'Merit marks for *Art*!' she said. 'I never got a merit mark for *Art* in me life.' Penny Weston didn't share number one brain rating with Raju Mistry for nothing. She studied the scrap of paper and she knew instantly what had been going on.

Kelvin knew she knew. Kelvin felt very ill but just stood there doing nothing, shirt gluey, palms oozing. Would she turn tail straightaway, charge for the staff-room and summon forth the Head of Bosworth House?

But no! Penny just stood there too, gazing at Kelvin with undisguised amazement, and, bit by bit, admiration. At last she shook her head and laid a hand on his boiled ham of an arm. 'Brilliant!' she said. 'You're brilliant!' and she set off backwards towards the classroom, pausing every now and then to shake her head and intone 'Brilliant!' in notes of deep awe.

Before Mr Warner dismissed Two Bosworth for the Christmas holidays he told them to give careful thought to who should be Form Captain next term. 'It must be someone,' he said sternly, as all eyes turned to the naughtiest girl in the class, 'who will bring *credit* to the House. Someone who will help us clinch that Achievement Cup.' Reluctantly all eyes slid instead towards Penny and Raju. Raju tried hard to straighten out his mouth. But Penny appeared not to notice that any eyes were on her. Her eyes were on Kelvin and they had a very thoughtful look in them. On the way out she did a good deal of whispering and a lot of people stared. Kelvin felt very sticky indeed.

When Mr Warner took nominations for Form Captain at the beginning of the spring term, he was very surprised indeed. The first person to be nominated was Kelvin Grant. 'Oh, come on,' said Mr Warner. 'We want some sensible nominations.' Penny Weston's hand waved like a banner. 'Yes, Penny? Who do you want to nominate?' 'I don't, Sir,' said Penny in her Managing Director voice. 'You're not being democratic, Sir. You've not asked for a seconder for Kelvin, and I second Kelvin, Sir.' 'Yeah, we second Kelvin, Sir,' came a third, fourth, fifth, sixth up to twenty-seventh voice.

There was simply no contest. Nobody else was nominated, though Raju Mistry did ask if you could nominate yourself. Nobody would second him, though. When it came to hands up, every single hand was raised for Kelvin and most of them were stabbing wildly. Faced with such a bristling armoury, there was nothing Mr Warner could do. Kelvin Grant became Form Captain of Two Bosworth by unanimous decision and the talk of the staff-room for at least a minute and a half.

Kelvin floated through the next few days as if on a great rubber duck. He floated home to tell his mother, he floated up to the Headmaster to receive his badge, he bobbed about on the warm sparkling water of the other children's friendship and approval. All the effort he'd put into getting his forgeries right had improved his spelling no end. His teachers congratulated themselves and *even awarded Kelvin merit marks*. He won six in one week and didn't once think about forgery.

But after those first few wonderful days Kelvin found himself growing very depressed. He didn't want to forge merit marks any longer. It was so much better winning them. What's more, words had now stopped jigging about quite so much, and he found that if he did it out loud to slow himself down *he could actually read quite OK*. Kelvin began to do his homework. And then he began to *enjoy* doing his homework. And then he started staying up half the night trying to win enough merit marks never to have to forge any ever again. But the strain was telling. His mam was dead worried about him and began talking to the neighbours about brainstorms. She was an easygoing woman. All the work that Kelvin was now putting in was making her feel uncomfortable. As his scratch became a hummock on the merit mark chart and his hummock began to heave up into a mountain, so the flesh began to fall off Kelvin. His mother muttered darkly to the neighbours, ''Snot only a *brainstorm*. I think our Kelv's caught that, you know, *anoraksia*.'

And, of course, the day dawned when Trafalgar House actually drew alongside. And then crept ahead.

The class fell upon Kelvin like hyenas. It happened at Break. Five barred the exit, and five drew the blinds down, and five plus five made a circle round about, and five raised their rulers on high. Then Penny Weston entered the arena, judge and jury and without mercy both. 'You're not doing it, are you? You can't be, or we'd win. You're *just not doing it*.' At length Kelvin hid his face in his hands, wept and agreed.

Penny Weston took immediate command. While one pinioned Kelvin's arms and two fettered his legs, she frisked him personally for merit mark slips. Then she stood over Kelvin and prodded him with a pair of compasses while he forged. And forged and forged. Penny collected the slips into bundles. 'This bunch this week, Trevor,' she said, doling them out. 'That's next week's lot, Hazel. And that, Wayne, is for the week after that.'

By the next count, Bosworth House had gone kangarooing into the lead. The second week, they slid into overdrive.

The third week's performance resembled the winner's at Le Mans. In a historic staff meeting the head of Trafalgar House threw down the gauntlet. He demanded a recount. The words that he used to make his demand caused the older members of staff to mutter about dismissal for unprofessional conduct. But the head of Trafalgar stayed on.

The old merit mark slips were kept in brown manilla envelopes, one for each week of the term. The head of Trafalgar and the head of Bosworth stood over these as over a brace of pistols for duelling at dawn. The Senior Mistress was umpire. She declared the contents of the first two envelopes to be in perfect order and the Head of Bosworth House hitched his top lip above his eye tooth.

But then somebody opened the third. First the head of Trafalgar pointed noiselessly to a slip that murmured Toe Boswort. Then to one that hiccuped Tow Bsowroht. Then to one that spluttered Wto Sbothrow. And finally to one that screamed forth Wot Sobwrot! And the truth was out . . .

That night Kelvin blew the dust from the Death List. He wrote a drum roll of names and added a firmament of stars. At the head of the roll call was the name of Penny Weston. Kelvin looked at it for a long time. Then he reached down the side of his bed and pulled out a large purple envelope.

He had bought it as soon as they appeared in the shops, the week after Penny Weston had clinched his appointment as Form Captain. Slowly he drew out the card.

It had a girl on the front, with a lot of spiky red hair and a large shocking pink heart throbbing through her school uniform. On the top of the card it had HEAD GIRL in big red letters. Underneath it said, 'Your heart's as big as your b . . .', and when you opened it up it read '. . . rain.'

Kelvin looked at it for a moment, then with a snigger he ripped it straight across. He flung it on the ground and jumped on it three times before stretching out his club of an arm towards the bag of doughnuts on his bed . . .

4
BIOLOGY LESSON

Leroy climbed the stairs, carrying his sports bag which contained his schoolbooks, kit, and last week's copy of *Healthy Living* magazine. He bought the magazine each week from Norval at great expense, after Norval had finished lending it round the class for a small charge. Leroy had told Norval that he was pricing himself out of the market.

'They're always defaced, boy. You don't pay much for soiled merchandise.'

Norval told Leroy he could buy the magazine elsewhere, but he wasn't lowering the price. 'No way.' Leroy continued to pay over the top.

'Where you goin', Leroy?' shouted his mam from the front room as she heard the stairs creak. She came out into the hall and said in a loud whisper, 'Don't bother wake up the baby, you 'ear what me say?' Leroy shared a room with the baby, five months. It was boring.

'I'm goin' to do my homework,' hissed back Leroy, banging his sports bag with his hand. 'Where'm I supposed to go?'

'You could come back now,' his mother called huskily back. 'Telly's down low. What's wrong wi' de livin' room?'

'Got to *concentrate*, ain't I?' growled Leroy. 'I'll keep real quiet. Won' disturb him.' And he swung round the banister at the top of the stairs and gently pushed open the door of the back bedroom. There was a light click. Leroy quietly closed the door behind him. His mam had a habit of creeping around! He didn't want to be disturbed.

The curtains were drawn. Leroy tiptoed to them and pulled one across slowly, wincing as it scraped. Now he could see his little brother, lying on his back, one tiny fist in his mouth, the other clenched beside him on the pillow. Leroy grinned. Nothing would wake him now. He was a great little sleeper – once he'd quit screaming! Leroy turned his attention to the job in hand. Out came football shirt, shorts (stiff with mud – time his mam washed those – better give them to her, come to think of it – he didn't want her poking around for them), socks (smelly, yuk), Geography book, because it was the biggest, for cover, and hidden in the centre pages, last week's copy of *Healthy Living* magazine. Great!

The late evening sun fell on the window-sill, creeping over the railway embankment, furry with willow-herb seed. It shone on the dead flies that lay where the sill joined the window. Leroy wondered idly why there were always dead flies. His mam was a careful cleaner. That meant flies must always be dying, the old corpses being replaced. Why did flies always die by the window? Did they go crazy trying to get out, exhaust themselves, and fall backwards, waving frantic legs till their hearts gave out? Did flies have hearts? Poor sods, battering and struggling against the glass trying to get to the sun. Leroy knew the feeling! Stuck in some classroom while the sun shone outside, high above the scanty shrubs and straggling trees in what they called 'the garden' at school – what a joke that was – while lorries shrieked and grumbled just outside the window and he longed to shriek and grumble with them. How come, when there was all that sun outside, none ever got into the classroom during Maths?

A train shuddered by. Leroy remembered *Healthy Living* magazine. Why waste time on thoughts of school when you could be looking at pictures of girls with no clothes on, enjoying themselves in the sun? Leroy wondered whether him and Norval could go to one of them back to nature places for their holidays this year. Nah, who was he kiddin'? They'd never let you, at twelve. Leroy grinned.

He could just imagine his mam's face if he casually said one day, 'Oh, Mam, I won't be goin' Mablethorpe with you this year. I'm goin' to this nuddy place with my mate Norval.'

Leroy opened the centre spread. She was somethin'! Wearing nothing but a flower in her hair and grinning at him over a slice of water-melon. She was as pretty as Vicky at school. Now there was a nice girl! But Norval was after her too. And as for Vicky herself, her green eyes were all over the place. And that smile! He'd got the full blast of it in Maths this morning . . .

At that moment Leroy heard the living-room door open. But his mam went through to the kitchen. Then there was the sound of her footsteps in the hall and coming up the stairs. Leroy hurriedly wrapped *Healthy Living* magazine in his football sweater and shoved it into his bag. He picked up the Geography book. His mam came into the room, whispering to him to go to the Asian shop and get her a pint of milk. 'Someone musta' drink the milk before I come in from work, Leroy.' Leroy groaned. 'But I'm *real* interested in this here Geography, Mam.'

The next day in school brought with it Biology, first two periods. Leroy made for his tall stool at the far back corner of the room, as far as possible from the teacher. Nothing personal. It was just school that bugged him. Miss Turner came in. 'Right,' she said breezily. 'Vicky, here are the exercise books.' She flung them down on the front bench. 'And, Kevin, would you give out the textbooks, please? Over there, side bench. Yes, that's right.' Vicky handed Leroy his exercise book and gave him a big wink. He smiled at her. Then he noticed Miss Turner had written a message, and drawn an enormous circle in red pen round the 'Leroy 4 Vicky' on the front of his book. He looked at this through narrowed eyes, then prodded Glen in the small of the back. Glen turned round, scowling.

'Lend us your red felt tip.'

Dutifully Glen passed it over. Miss Turner yelled at him for turning round. Glen went red and huddled into his work like a frightened guinea-pig burrowing into straw. He began to copy the diagram that Miss Turner was drawing on the board, very earnestly.

Miss Turner liked everything to be clean and clear of mess, from bench tops to books. If any pupil expressed himself on an exercise book cover, then the self-expression had to be encased in clean, clear paper, immediately. But Leroy wasn't any pupil. He was a pupil in love. So where Miss Turner had written in big letters 'Back this book' underneath the 'Leroy 4 Vicky', Leroy wrote 'No' in equally big letters and began to block them in. When he'd done that, he took a careless look at the diagram on the board. It looked dead complicated and boring. He'd start it in a minute. He rummaged in his sports bag for a scrap of paper, found one and began a note to Vicky. 'How about a little cuddle?' it said. It looked a bit plain. He gave it a border of hearts, working very carefully. When at last he had finished, he made it into a paper dart. Then he waited until Miss Turner had just turned from her notes back to the board, and stood up, took careful aim, and hurled it.

It landed on Smelly Lesley's desk, next but one from Vicky. Leroy swore to himself and hastily began work on the diagram, head well down. The kids who had witnessed the progress of the dart turned round in astonishment to see who was chucking messages at Smelly Lesley. Lesley herself snatched up the dart, looking quickly backwards, a frown on her face, to see who was insulting her this time. She unravelled the note and couldn't believe her eyes when she read what it said. She turned around again, face aglow, in the hope of meeting the eyes of her unknown admirer. She was very disappointed. All heads were firmly down.

Leroy, having nothing better to do, continued with the diagram. It was of the ear. Dead boring! He gave up and flicked through the pages of the textbook, in search of something more interesting. But he already knew it was a waste of time. He had turned to the section on reproduction with the greatest enthusiasm the first time. They all had. But what a let-down! Only a few boring diagrams of eggs and sperm and the insides of men and women and babies growing from tadpoles to gnomes, and a load about the rabbit! Why was sex in school always about babies and rabbits? There wasn't a single baby in *Healthy Living* magazine. Or a rabbit, come to that!

Leroy continued to turn pages. Here was a picture of a skeleton. Bones! Bones was boring. The skeleton looked as if it could be a man or a woman. Time he gave it a bit of human interest. A woman. He gave her plenty of Afro hair and placed a big red flower in it. He gave her a large chunk of water-melon to eat. He gave her beautiful pear-shaped bosoms. He was so intent on his work, the tip of his tongue out of the side of his mouth in concentration, that he didn't notice that Miss had reached the back of the room, bending over everybody's book to inspect their diagrams. When he heard the light tap, tap of her heels approaching him, he panicked for a moment, banged the textbook shut, flung down the felt tip, snatched up his ballpoint, and gazed at the board with the greatest attention.

'Leroy Hall!' cried Miss Turner in exasperation. 'What *have* you been doing all morning? I saw you bang your textbook shut. You're supposed to be copying from the board, not the textbook. I told you last week that the diagram in there is misleading. Don't you ever listen? And you shouldn't be drawing in biro. In pencil, always in pencil. Where's your pencil, Leroy?'

'Haven't-got-one-Miss,' mumbled Leroy.

'*Who's* got a pencil Leroy could borrow?' cried Miss Turner, heel tapping. There were plenty of offers, specially from the girls. Vicky jumped up and came running to the back, holding out a jumbo pencil with a great fat rubber on the end. Again she winked at Leroy.'I don't think *that's* very helpful, Vicky,' said Miss Turner, her mouth crinkling at the edges. 'I don't think Leroy will do very *neat* diagrams with a monster like that. Who's got a pencil of a more *suitable* size?' A more modest pencil was passed.

'Right,' said Miss Turner. 'Two more minutes should be plenty for those who've been working properly. The rest, Leroy, will have to stay in at Break and finish then.'

'Oh, Miss,' moaned Leroy. 'I've got a soccer meeting at Break.'

Miss Turner shrugged. 'That's your problem, Leroy,' she said. 'You should have thought of that when you chose to waste time in *my* lesson. Right, everybody, that's time enough, I think. Glen, would you start reading for us from page thirty-nine in the textbook, please? From the heading "The Ear".'

Leroy was fuming. Miss Turner was rotten. He was glad he'd messed up her stupid old textbook. He'd show her . . .

It was a week later. Biology again! It hadn't been a particularly good week. One visit to the Head for fighting in the yard – and they'd only been playing! One to the Deputy for wearing his woolly hat, scarf and pilot jacket

round school. God, you couldn't do anything. Someone
was always spying on you or grassing on you. Leroy made
his way to his usual back corner and threw himself on to his
stool, putting his head down on his arms.

Miss Turner came in. Leroy raised his head. She didn't
look very pleased. In fact, she looked in a very bad mood.
In fact, she looked bloody furious. Oh, God, what was it
this time?

'Right, second years,' she said. 'Something very serious
has happened, and I know one of you is to blame. Nobody
will be leaving this room until that someone has owned
up.' Leroy felt his stomach lurch. He knew what it would
be. Miss Turner strode across the room and picked up a
biology textbook. She flounced back to her desk, heels
clicking like crazy. She paused dramatically for effect,
holding the book up and twitching it. She started rather
low. 'I happened to flick through one or two of these last
week after your lesson,' she said. 'No other class has used
them since last term and they were all quite all right then.'
Her voice rose. 'Someone in this class had *defaced* one of
these very expensive textbooks.'

The class brightened up immediately. They'd hoped
that's what it might be. They stretched their necks in
anticipation. Now Miss would show them. That should be
good for a laugh!

But Miss Turner had not been born yesterday. She might
be new to teaching but she was not new to kids. She was
the oldest of six. She knew how their minds worked. She
knew that the moment of truth had arrived, the oldest,
bloodiest battle in the book – Class versus New Teacher.
Her dark eyes shone. She rose to the full peak of her five
foot one inch. She was ready for anything.

The class was at fever pitch. They longed now for her to

show them so that they could let rip in the loudest roar of laughter that had been heard in the building since Class versus Mr Simpson two terms ago. (Mr Simpson had since given up teaching and gone to work in the local government offices.)

Miss Turner lifted the book on high. Thirty-two pairs of eyes followed it on the way up. Then she hurled it down on to her desk with the whole of her five foot one inch behind it. It fell flat with a tremendous smack. The class rose about three inches into the air.

It was then that Miss Turner really let rip. The class would never have believed that so much noise could come from such a very small person. Glen winced and, without thinking, put his hands over his ears.

'Whoever did this is going to *own up*, do you hear? If we stay here all night he or she is going to own up. Yes, Sarah, what is it? It surely wasn't *you*, was it?'

Sarah Baines shook her head until her ribbons fluttered. What a cheek! Just wait until her mam heard *that*. 'Please, Miss Turner, you're not allowed to keep us after four o'clock. Not without our parents having twenty-four hours' notice, you're not.' She looked round triumphantly at the rest of the class to back her up. They nodded doubtfully. Yes, that was right. But that was only a rule. And when teachers got as mad as Miss Turner was today, rules just disappeared into thin air. When you saw somebody as mad as that, it didn't surprise you one little bit that some people could bend forks just by looking at them!

'There won't be any need for you to stay here beyond half-past *ten*, Sarah,' said Miss Turner in a grim voice, 'if the person who defaced the book owns up. And I want that person to know that I think spoiling school property is bad enough but that being a coward and making others suffer is far worse.'

Leroy wriggled in his chair. He didn't feel very well. He wondered if he could say he felt sick, could he go home now, please? But that would immediately show him up as the one who did it. What was he going to *do*?

Miss Turner said that the class was to work quietly on its own that morning. She handed out work sheets quickly, face like stone. 'This will give the guilty party,' she said coldly, 'a chance to come and have a little chat with me outside the door.'

The class sighed and wriggled and settled down to their work. Ten o'clock came. The class worked absolutely quietly – no whispering, no giggling. They only paused to glance at the clock now and again, throw Miss Turner a worried look and return with a great show of earnestness to their work again, throwing the occasional look heaven-wards too, as if to beam in to extra-terrestrial inspiration.

Quarter-past ten came. The class stirred ever so slightly and glanced at one another and threw a few eyebrows up in certain directions. Twenty past ten.

Leroy was in a cold sweat. He couldn't own up. They'd tell his parents and they'd be so disgusted with him. They'd think he was rude. Miss Turner would think he was rude. She would tell the Head. All the teachers would know. They'd all know he was rude. He was very sorry now that he'd done it. He could have drawn on a scrap of paper out of his bag instead. There was already quite a nice collection of cartoons showing the adventures of a girl with no clothes on and wearing a flower in her hair. He could have added to that. He'd never thought of it being rude before but *they'd* think so, the grown-ups. Perhaps this was some sort of punishment for him, from God, for being rude. But was it rude? He didn't know. But it *was* bad to spoil a schoolbook. He wished he hadn't. It was only because he'd been bored. School!

The clock jerked to twenty-five past ten. Leroy stared straight ahead. He didn't move a muscle.

The bell rang. There was a sort of whistle from the class as of the wind in the chimney. Miss Turner looked up from her work, face white and strained. 'Right, second years,' she said. 'No Break for any of you. I'm going to get my coffee so stay right here and I'll be straight back.' There was a howl of protest. 'Nobody needs to stay all Break if whoever is to blame owns up. If not, then back you all come at quarter to four.'

Miss Turner prayed long and hard on her way to the staff-room that someone would own up. If the clock jerked to four o'clock and they were all sitting around like stuffed monkeys she'd be in a difficult position. 'Ah, well. Cross that bridge when you come to it,' she thought. She would take a long time getting her coffee. Take a leisurely trip to the ladies. Let a little bit of pressure from the others build up. That could work miracles . . .

Back in the Biology lab. the pressure was on. On Norval to begin with. There had been a case like this before. Geography book, that time. A native of Australia, as naked as nature intended, had been made a little larger in all directions (even to her nose) than had quite been nature's intent. She had also suddenly sprouted large specs and a handlebar moustache. It had to be Norval again.

'Tell her, you prat,' hissed Sarah. 'Else we'll all be kept in. Tell her, Norval. Go on!'

'It *weren't* me,' hissed back the long-suffering Norval. 'Not this time, it weren't.' Sarah looked suspicious but decided to believe him. She turned on other likely characters. All, in tones of hurt indignation, echoed the same message. 'It weren't me. Not this time.'

At last someone thought of Leroy. In fact, it was Norval. 'It would be!' thought Leroy, so mad at Norval's betrayal of him that it made him feel that he wasn't really to blame and that in some strange way Norval was. For this reason he had no difficulty in hotly denying the charge. He almost believed himself.

Miss Turner returned. No one, naturally, owned up. The bell rang for the end of Break. Miss Turner looked grimmer than ever. 'Right!' she said. 'It's the end of school then. I shall take a register. If anyone doesn't turn up, I shall take it that they are to blame.' She said nothing about not being able to keep them after four o'clock. Sarah considered bringing the subject up again, but thought better of it, Miss Turner looked that mad.

The storm broke outside. Norval, seeing the way Leroy looked at him, laid the blame firmly on Leroy again. He decided that attack was the best form of defence. Besides, he was pretty certain Leroy *was* to blame. He'd got told off for having his textbook open, hadn't he? The kids sent Leroy poison-pen letters all through Maths. He was soon in trouble with the teacher. Maths wasn't his strong subject at the best of times and when he kept receiving little messages about being beaten up and stuffed down the bog, well, how could he concentrate on vulgar fractions?

At twelve o'clock when the bell went again Leroy tore from the classroom to the room where the dinner register was taken, to seek the protection of the member of staff on duty. Unfortunately that member of staff was late arriving and turned out to be Miss Turner! By the time she did come there were tears in Leroy's eyes. They were tears of pain! Miss Turner chose not to notice.

As the dinner hour went on Leroy slowly came to the conclusion that he would have to own up. He decided this in the middle of eating his sponge pudding and the decision caused a most terrible heaving of the gut that nearly made him throw up. Back in the yard he was tormented again. He noticed with pain that even Vicky joined in the tormenting. At that point he gave in, confessed, promised he'd go to Miss Turner as soon as the bell went at the end of afternoon school and told the others they needn't show up. The others cheered.

How he got through that afternoon he would never know. It seemed to pass in a haze of pain and guilt and dread. What was going to happen to him?

Quarter to four found him trembling outside Miss Turner's door, waiting for her to dismiss the Fourth Year. To his amazement they looked as if they were having a good laugh with her. The smile hadn't left her face when he nervously knocked and went in. It soon did, though, when she saw him. 'Yes, Leroy?' she said. 'Are you the first? Where are all the others?' She frowned in anger that they were late.

'They're not coming, Miss,' Leroy gulped. 'It was me, Miss. I did it. I'm ever so sorry, Miss. Honest. I'll never do it again.'

Miss Turner didn't shout. She didn't even look any crosser. In fact, if anything, she looked less cross. 'Come over here, Leroy,' she said. 'Shut the door behind you.' She spoke quite gently but he noticed that she was opening the textbook at a page marked with a slip of paper. Oh, no, she was going to make him look at what he'd drawn in front of her. How horrible! Slowly he went over to her. 'All right, Leroy,' she said. 'Take a good look at your artwork now and tell me just one thing. Why it's necessary to spoil a perfectly good book that other children are going to have to use. Try and see it as others will see it and then tell me what you've got to say on the matter.'

Slowly Leroy made his eyes travel to the page. They didn't really want to move. They slid this way and that, trying to escape. He felt hot and sweaty and sick. At last his eyes reached the offending picture.

And Leroy had no problem about seeing the picture as others would see it. He had no problem at all. Because *it wasn't his picture!*

It was far worse than his had ever been. For a start the skeleton had been made into a man, not a woman. (Oh, yes, it was the same page. It was the same skeleton diagram. But it wasn't *his* skeleton picture.) The man was grotesque, enormous, totally exaggerated. It was disgusting! Leroy gave a gasp of surprise and horror.

But he couldn't say anything. He just couldn't. If he said it wasn't his, it wouldn't solve anything. She'd only want to see the one that he'd done. But she thought that he'd done *this*! He wouldn't want other kids seeing *this*. But then he wouldn't want other kids seeing his, either. He'd never even thought of other people seeing it. He hadn't thought at all, except that he felt bored. And fed up because his note for Vicky had landed on Smelly Lesley's desk . . .

'What is it, Leroy?' said Miss Turner at last, a little anxiously, surprised by the gasp he had given and looking at the boy's eyes which were wide with real horror.

'N . . . nothing, Miss,' gasped Leroy. If he told the truth, somebody else'd be for it and it'd be grassing. Mind you, whoever it was deserved it. Making him take the blame like that. If he knew who it was . . . Norval! He bet it was Norval all along. He'd get that prat . . .

Miss Turner snapped the book shut. 'Well now, Leroy,'

she said briskly. 'I think you've had punishment enough as a result of a very silly incident. That drawing doesn't belong to the real world, now, does it? Can you see that it could upset and offend people in the real world? Can you see that, Leroy?'

Leroy nodded, the tears beginning to creep out of the corners of his eyes. Miss Turner seemed to sense they were there, even though he had his head well down. 'Now don't cry,' she said kindly. 'We'll say no more about it. I shall cut that page out. It won't matter, just one page. And then I shall forget all about it. And you must, too. Just remember, Leroy, to try to live a little bit more in the real world from now on, where there's work to be done. You can practise your drawing at home.' She gave him a grin and patted him on the shoulder. 'Go along now.'

Leroy sped off. She wasn't going to tell his parents! She wasn't going to tell anyone! And, yes, he would try to forget. Thank God! But fancy her thinking he'd drawn *that*. He just had one more thing to do before he could forget. Wait till he saw Norval tomorrow morning . . .

Leroy was in the playground early next morning. But someone was there even earlier! It was Vicky! What was she doing there? It wasn't like Vicky to be early. He forgot about Norval. But when Vicky looked up and saw him coming towards her, she turned away and began to run towards the girls-only area and the bogs. What was she doing that for? She couldn't be that desperate to go. Leroy felt cross and hurt. He remembered how she'd betrayed him yesterday. 'Vicky!' he shouted angrily. 'Come back here.' But she didn't stop. And she didn't come out of the bogs until it was time to line up.

Leroy was furious. And Norval hadn't shown up. But if

Leroy had stopped to think about it, he would have remembered that Norval always came late. He was always standing outside the Headmaster's room, lolling up against the wall, when the other kids were going to first lesson.

When Leroy caught sight of Vicky in the girls' line he noticed with a shock that it looked as if she'd been crying. 'Vicky!' he whispered across at her anxiously. She shot him a frightened little look but didn't reply.

And suddenly a most awful thought crossed Leroy's mind. That picture yesterday – it had been of a man! Now why should Norval draw a *man*? An idea was taking shape in Leroy's mind. He took another look across at Vicky. Yes, she carried a school bag. Not a sports bag like his but one of those blue canvas efforts girls carry with Snoopy on it.

In Maths, Leroy made sure that he sat behind Vicky instead of in his usual place at the back. He noticed that she glanced nervously round when he took his place, but she didn't make any comment. Neither did he. But he felt more certain than ever. Her bag was lying in the gangway. Great. He put out his foot. She was deep in her work – or her thoughts! He slid his foot as far forward as he could and managed to hook it into the handle. Still she didn't look up. He pulled it towards him slowly.

He had it at last! Quickly he lifted it on to his knee and felt around inside. Books, a jumper, toffees, scraps of paper. He pulled one or two out. Nothing very interesting. One had names of pop stars and football players on, and lots of working out, and at the bottom 'Vicky loves Kevin Keegan'. Leroy grinned, but it wasn't what he was looking for. He felt again, pulled out a sheaf of papers and, yes, this was it. An enormous naked man stared up at him, just like the one in the Biology book!

At that moment Vicky reached down to get out her ruler from her bag. She groped for it, looked down for it, then swivelled round as quick as thought. Leroy held up the picture for a moment and raised his eyebrows.

He couldn't help grinning at her, she looked that scared. Then she looked as if she was going to cry. He blew her a kiss. And at last she grinned at him, a worried grin, but a grin all the same.

And Leroy grinned harder than ever. Because now he knew that if he was rude, so was Vicky! It wasn't only lads then! Vicky was *very* rude! Much ruder than him, in fact. His smile broadened. To hell with words like rude. They meant nothing. He liked girls. He liked Vicky! He wasn't ashamed of himself any more.

And Vicky grinned back at him, a bigger grin than ever. Bigger by far than he'd ever seen her grin at that prat Norval . . .

5
CINDY ASHTON
IS VERY THIN

Cindy Ashton was very special right from the start. Cindy's mum was forty-four when Cindy was born. Her dad was forty-six. Cindy was their only child. 'Our little girl,' Cindy's parents would say proudly to anyone who'd listen. 'Our little girl Cindy.'

When little girl Cindy was fourteen and the girls in her class wore ra-ra skirts on week-ends, smoked in the school bogs, carved chunks out of their arms if they couldn't go to Adam Ant concerts and fell in love with the entire band of Duran Duran, Cindy was still wearing short white socks and shoes with bars across, just like Mrs Ashton did when she was a little girl. 'I don't want my Cindy mixing with those awful girls from that terrible school,' said Mrs Ashton to Cindy. 'They're so *common*.' So at Break time and dinner time Cindy walked round and round the edge of the playground, like an ant round a cake-board, all on her own, telling herself that she didn't like cake *anyway*.

The only person Cindy ever talked to was the Miss on yard duty. 'Zena Wardle's smoking in the toilets again, Miss,' she would say, the rare times she risked a visit in that direction. All the Misses looked hastily the other way as soon as they saw Cindy creeping into view. They didn't like Cindy any more than the girls did. 'That Cindy,' said the Headmistress, 'makes my flesh crawl.' Some of the teachers looked shocked. But they all knew what she meant.

One cold blustery November morning Miss Pool was on duty. She hadn't wanted to go outside. She'd stayed in the staff-room dragging on her cigarette until long after the bell. The Senior Master had had to look at his watch and look at the clock and look at Miss Pool three times before Miss Pool had taken the hint. Now she stood in the yard, shivering and complaining, her hands clasped round her mug of coffee as if in prayer, her knees bent and twitching, and her head snuggled as far down as she could get it into Great Aunt Bertha Jane's fur coat.

'Least you can wear *trousers*, Miss,' shuddered Zena Wardle. She had on a striped cotton jacket that the Headmistress would confiscate when she saw it. She wore this over her school skirt which she had shortened by turning it over five times at the hem, like a pelmet edged with a sausage. 'T'ain't *fair*.'

At that moment Miss Pool felt someone touch the side of Great Aunt Bertha Jane's fur, then stroke it. She was used to this. The first years did it all the time. She glanced round, but it wasn't a first year. She looked into the pale little-girl face of Cindy Ashton. Zena caught sight of her too, and zigzagged off, moving her weight from one hip to the other like a road walker.

Miss Pool took a frosty breath, ready to snap at Cindy as soon as she pointed out another rule broken. It was probably Zena's jacket this time. Miss Pool ought to send Zena home to change it. But she knew that if she did, they wouldn't see Zena for a week, maybe two.

But then Cindy gave her a shock. 'I'm shrinking, Miss,' said Cindy, very matter-of-fact, her pink-rimmed, sleep-edged, watery eyes on the mobiles, her hand still stroking the fur.

Miss Pool felt like someone had just shoved an ice cube between her angora jumper and her thermal vest. 'Don't be silly, Cindy,' she snapped, to give herself time to think. 'I am, though, Miss,' said Cindy. 'I'm shrinking.'

'What do you mean, Cindy?' said Miss Pool, forcing herself to look at Cindy for the first time in months. She was as thin as a carrot. Miss Pool thought she knew what Cindy meant.

Cindy shrugged. 'I'm shrinking, Miss,' she repeated, her ferret eyes still on the mobiles. One hand stroked Miss Pool's coat and the other crumpled her school skirt which drooped fifteen centimetres beneath her regulation school mac to allow Room for Growth.

Miss Pool tried very hard not to rip Great Aunt Bertha Jane's fur away from Cindy's stroke, stroke, stroke. The first years stroked hurriedly and guiltily twice, three, four times, then shrieked and ran away. Cindy looked like she'd stroke the coat, fix the mobiles with her pale eyes and complain that she was shrinking till they all turned to stone. But Zena Wardle was swivelling back again and Cindy shuffled off on her knitting-needle legs, ploughing through the material of her long blue skirt like through four-foot waves. She wasn't shrinking in *length*, certainly. She looked more like a stick insect pacing out a cake-board these days. Cindy Ashton was very very thin.

Two weeks later Miss Pool was on duty again. The weather had got steadily colder. Miss Pool now wore her thermal vest, long johns, trousers, angora sweater, a mohair cardigan, a padded waistcoat, Great Aunt Bertha Jane's fur, and a scarf wrapped five times round her neck and trailing, like Dr Who. This walking igloo was topped by a balaclava rounded off with a cossack hat. Zena Wardle's striped blazer had been confiscated the day before. She now wore a gold nylon zipper jacket and looked like she'd got the belly-ache, she was so doubled over with cold. Miss Pool decided that skiving was better than treble pneumonia and packed her off home.

Miss Pool had completely forgotten about Cindy Ashton until now when she felt that stroke, stroke, stroke once more. She shuddered beneath her layers as she saw again those pale distant eyes and heard the dead little voice drone,

'I'm shrinking, Miss. I am. I'm shrinking.' Miss Pool looked at Cindy. Her skirt seemed to droop longer than ever beneath her school mac, two bones stuck out of her face beneath the watery eyes, her thin hair seemed glued to her skull. Miss Pool felt very worried indeed.

She went to see the Headmistress before Assembly. 'I'm worried about Cindy Ashton, Mrs Carr,' she said, unwinding herself from the scarf like a mummy cloth. 'She insists she's *shrinking*. And I think she has a point.'

She described to Mrs Carr what Cindy looked like these days. Mrs Carr couldn't say she'd noticed. Like everybody else Mrs Carr didn't look at Cindy Ashton more than was absolutely necessary. 'Only child of elderly parents, isn't she?' said Mrs Carr. 'Made much of? Spoilt brat?'

'Well, they will insist she's their *little* girl,' said Miss Pool. She remembered now a Parents' Evening and Cindy's parents bending in too close, rubbing their hands together and saying, 'Our *little* girl. Our little girl Cindy.' Cindy had cowered back in her chair, trying to pass herself off as the Invisible Woman.

'Mmm. Emotionally Backward,' said Mrs Carr, putting her fingers together and looking efficient. 'A clear candidate for a Small Group, wouldn't you say?' Small Groups were Mrs Carr's very favourite. 'Then we can take a really close look at her.' Mrs Carr's subject was Biology. She made Cindy sound like a sliver on a slab. 'Which year is she in?'

'Third year, Mrs Carr,' said Miss Pool doubtfully. She knew what sort of children were taught in Small Groups. They were cheeky and noisy and backward (at lessons) and fought a lot and were mostly boys. Among that shower Cindy would not so much shrink as curl up and die!

But Mrs Carr was determined. She hadn't placed an

Emotionally backward child in a Small Group before, only the Educationally Backward. It seemed to do them a great deal of good. They left school at the earliest possible opportunity, which suited everybody just fine. They didn't come within five thousand miles of taking any exams, or indeed of the school if they could help it. And they ended up running strings of dry cleaners or betting shops or Space Invader parlours, and changing their cars when the ashtray got full. They gave lots of money to the school in later years, in grateful memory of the beatings they'd received when being Formed.

'Third year. That's Mr Arbuthnot,' said Mrs Carr. 'He'll see she's all right.'

Miss Pool felt more worried than ever. The trouble was that Mr Arbuthnot was now so old and tired that he'd stopped noticing when things were entirely wrong. He'd been a good teacher once, when he was young and burning with love for his scruffy Small Groups. In those days he'd yelled the kids cheerfully into doing what he wanted and they'd yelled cheerfully back. Lessons were conducted at the highest decibel rate the human voice is capable of. With no harm to anyone. Except that those not used to Small Groups fell back about ten paces when they first met them. Mr Arbuthnot had cuffed his kids in fun and his kids had cheeked Mr Arbuthnot in fun and everyone was as happy as the day-didn't-seem-too-long. Those were the days when Mr Arbuthnot's former pupils drove Mr Arbuthnot to school by Mercedes-Benz before going off to Ladbroke's and a day at the races.

But those days were no more.

Kids were now always at the staff-room door saying where was Mr Arbuthnot because there was an uprising in the mobiles and Avninder Singh was spouting blood through his ears and Please-Sir-it-wasn't-*me*-Sir, but could Mr Arbuthnot come *quick*. They had to lever Mr Arbuthnot from his armchair by the radiator where he sat in his outdoor coat reading the paper, entirely surrounded by smokescreen. Mr Arbuthnot was even entirely surrounded by smokescreen in the classroom these days. Sometimes he could be spotted rearing up like the Loch Ness monster but only for a severed artery at the very least.

And Mr Arbuthnot was no longer cheerful. Rumour had it he had flung a kid against a wall and broken his arm. Mr Arbuthnot's Small Groups nowadays were shifty-eyed and sullen. They were more likely to end up behind the fort-like walls of the city jail than behind the leopard-skin wheel of a Mercedes-Benz.

The day came all too soon when Cindy Ashton was to join Mr Arbuthnot's Small Group. Cindy had looked half-crazed with fright when she heard what her fate was to be. Her parents too were very put out. 'What's all this about *shrinking*, Cindy?' demanded her father, removing his pork pie hat and pigskin driving gloves after an evening meeting with the Headmistress.

Cindy's pale eyes crossed with fright. 'I don't know what you're on about, Dad,' she said. She slid out of reach of his arm. It would have pulled her on to his knee. She gave the carpet some study-in-depth.

Mr Ashton gave his wife a triumphant look. 'There, Mother, what did I tell you?' He lit up his pipe and sucked, waving the match dangerously close to the standard lamp's fringed shade (with hunting scenes). 'What did I say to that damn stupid woman?'

Mrs Ashton quivered, remembering. 'Stuff and non-sense, Madam, with respect,' Mr Ashton had said. 'Our little girl Cindy would never make a daft remark like that.'

'But I'm afraid she did say *exactly* that, Mr Ashton,' the Headmistress had replied, giving Mr Ashton the over-the-spectacles look. 'And, you must admit, Cindy has lost an awful lot of weight.'

'She's shot up, that's all,' quavered Mrs Ashton, herself as thin as a pin. 'Our little girl looks a wee bit on the slim side because she's shooting up. Nothing wrong with that as I can see. It's growth.'

'If she's growing so much, Mrs Ashton,' snapped the Headmistress, 'she's your little girl no longer. Now is she?'

Mr Ashton held up his hand. '*I'll* answer that one, Mother,' he said to his wife. He turned with dignity to the Headmistress. 'To Mrs Ashton and myself,' said Mr Ashton, fixing the Headmistress with the end of his pipe, 'Cindy will always be our little girl.'

The Headmistress snorted and Mr Ashton signalled to his wife that the interview was at an end.

'I *never* said I was shrinking,' repeated Cindy, dogfish eyes popping though glazed. Mr Ashton nodded with every suck on his pipe and stretched out his Cindy arm to turn on 'Any Answers'. (He was always sending David Jacobs his point of view. So far he had not been far-sighted enough to broadcast it to a wondering and grateful nation.) 'We'll see what the Director of Education has to say about Small Groups for our little girl.'

Cindy shifted. 'Don't make a fuss, Dad,' she murmured. 'I don't want any fuss.' Her father silenced her with a wave of his pipe.

But if Cindy didn't want any fuss she had to go to school. And that meant the Small Group. The first time Cindy sidled into Mr Arbuthnot's classroom Imran Khan was garrotting Paul Alexander and Mr Arbuthnot was taking a snooze. The newspaper gently rose and fell

over by the radiator. Imran Khan ended up shoving Paul
Alexander so hard he shot half-way across the classroom.
He crash-landed on the newspaper and Mr Arbuthnot
rose like a vampire from a coffin. He snatched at the
paper and brandished it. He yelled and yelled in the
general direction of Imran Khan and Paul. At last the
reason for the shouting penetrated Imran's skull and he
dug Paul in the gut with his elbow. 'A fink 'e's speakin'
to you.' Cindy crept backwards into the chair Mr
Arbuthnot had just launched himself off. She took in the
scene through gobstopper eyes.

But soon Imran and Paul were seated side by side as if
the strangulation of the one by the other was as unlikely as
hailstones in June. Cindy was made to sit behind them,
next to Zena Wardle, while Mr Arbuthnot mumbled the
register. She heard Imran say, 'I saw Florio Zarconi last
night.'

'And?' said Paul.

''E was scrappin' wiv vis Greabo. Vis Greabo kep' callin'
Florio names and Florio, 'e says, "I'm Florio Zarconi. You
can't speak to *me* like vat." '

'And?'

'Vis Greabo, 'e got a bad bruise.'

Cindy shuddered. Imran turned round. 'What's your
name?' said Imran. Stuttering, Cindy told him. Imran
nodded. He turned back.

A moment later Imran turned round again. 'When your
muvver made you, Cindy Ashton,' he said, 'she made a
'orrible mistake.' Cindy started to cry . . .

Cindy and Zena Wardle were the only white girls in the
Small Group. There were three shy Asian girls who
chattered to one another in their own language and a West

Indian girl called Pauline. Imran and Paul made the same joke about her every morning.

'Where does Pauline come from?'

'Jamaica?'

'No, she let me.'

Then Pauline would set about them with her netball skirt.

The next day Imran had written in slanty letters across the blackboard: 'Sindy Ashtun is verry thin.' When Cindy had read it, Imran turned round to Zena. 'When your mam made you, Zena Wardle,' said Imran, 'she made a 'orrible mistake.' Zena jumped up and then Imran jumped up and Zena aimed a kick at where Imran's body joined his legs. Zena sat down again and said to Cindy, 'I *was* a mistake, see? A haccident. You know.' Cindy didn't know. But if Zena thought she was a mistake, then perhaps Zena would understand about Cindy shrinking . . .

Because Cindy knew she *was* shrinking. She'd wanted to tell Miss Pool about it. She'd thought she was nice, that Miss Pool. But all Miss Pool had done was get her stuck in this terrible horrible Small Group. Cindy kept close to Zena for the rest of the day.

It meant a load of trouble. Zena was always in trouble. By dinner time Mrs Carr had spotted and confiscated the gold nylon zip-up, and been on the receiving end of a barrel load of prime cheek, and Zena was On Report.

On Report meant you had to carry this blank timetable round and the teacher had to write at the end of each lesson how you'd been. Then you had to take it to the Headmistress at the end of the day. Zena's report said at the top, 'Comment on behaviour and dress'.

The first lesson after dinner was Science. Zena had gone home at dinner time to put on her leg-warmers as the

temperature was still dropping. She didn't wear a coat –
she hadn't got one. She wore a big hairy sweater instead.
Mr Arbuthnot didn't notice, of course, at Registration. But
Mr Peterson who took them for Science did! He blocked
Zena's way at the door. 'Divest yourself of those monstros-
ities, Zena.'

'Eh? Ugh? Y'wot?'

'Take your leg-warmers off.'

'Shan't.'

'Very well, then. Take yourself off home.' Mr Peterson
wasn't bothering with report forms. Nor with the chance
they might not see Zena for a week, maybe two. All the
better, in Mr Peterson's view.

'Aa-ah. But I wanna do hexperiments.'

'Well, of course you shall do experiments, Zena. *Just
take your leg-warmers off.*'

'T'ain't fair.' All the same Zena plonked herself down
there and then and peeled off the leg-warmers, showing a
lot of hitched-up purple long john under her sausage-edged
skirt. Mr Peterson groaned, veiling his eyes with his hands.
Zena chuntered to Cindy all through the expansion of
metal. 'Teachers can wear what *they* like. Women teachers
can wear trousers and all that. At my bruvver's school girls
wear trousers 'cos of their religion. I'm goin' on strike.
Will you go on strike wiv me, Cindy?'

It was the first time any kid had asked Cindy to do
anything. She turned pink, pulled back her shoulders, lifted
her head and shot up three inches. 'Yes, all right, Zena,'
she said.

'We'll go my 'ouse after school then,' said Zena. 'Make
banners and stuff.' Cindy was about to say that she wasn't
allowed to go to anybody's house, on account of them
being common, when it struck her how worried her mum

would be if she was late. Cindy vowed there and then to stay out till after her dad got home. She imagined her mum saying, 'Oh, Father, whatever can have happened to our little girl?' and her mouth twitched.

It wasn't very nice at Zena's. She only had a mam and her mam was out working and the house was cold and dark. Still, they had a great time making banners. Zena's said, 'Discriminashun. Lads and ancients wear trousers. Why can't grils?' Cindy looked at it. 'What do you mean, ancients?' she said.

'You know. *Ancients,*' said Zena. 'Imran and that lot.'

'You mean *Asians,*' said Cindy.

'S'what I said,' said Zena fiercely. 'Ancients.'

Cindy gave up. She concentrated on colouring in her own poster that said, 'Teachers DOWN. Leg-warmers UP.' Cindy even whistled. She didn't think she'd been so happy – ever. They stuck their posters on bamboo canes Zena had nicked from the hardware shop. 'I'd really *love* some leg-warmers,' said Cindy wistfully. 'I'll get you some,' said Zena straight off. 'I could do with some clean ones meself.' So they went up town and Zena kitted her out.

There was an awful row when Cindy got home. Her mum was crying and her dad did a lot of jabbing with the pipe and Cindy cheeked him for the first time ever and Cindy's mum had hysterics and her dad slapped Cindy and then slapped her mum. And Cindy was sent to bed without any tea. 'Because that's what happens to *rude* little girls.'

'It's that Small Group,' Cindy heard her dad say to her mum. 'This isn't our little girl, Mother. It's not our little girl at all.' Cindy hugged herself on the landing.

The next day was the coldest yet. It was once more the turn of Miss Pool to come on duty and she was late. Zena and Cindy paraded the playground with their banners and everyone charged up.

'You goin' on *strike* then, Zena?' they jabbered. 'You *too*, Cindy?' Nobody could believe it. 'Can we join in?' Zena went round marshalling pickets like she was choosing a rounders team. 'You can be. I'll 'ave you. Yes, you. Get lost, you. Not 'er. She's a scruff.'

Even the boys were interested. They crowded to the edge of the girls' yard. There was a lot of muttering and some of them ran out of school. By the time Miss Pool and Mr Peterson came on duty banners were sprouting like pimples. Some said, 'Who needs school?' and 'This is a dump' and 'Blow up Colditz', but others proclaimed 'Birdman of the Year' and 'Free Baz now' and 'Boogie till it hurts'.

Miss's eyes rabbit-hopped over the banners and kept returning to Cindy who was roosting on the ground next to Zena over by the mobiles. Her skirt had been chopped a good thirteen centimetres above the knee and not very straight at that and her spider's legs were fifty centimetres fatter all round, padded out as they were with four pairs of leg-warmers. A lime-green pair folded over to show a pink, yellow and orange stripey pair turned back to reveal a purple pair shot through with gold thread pushed down to disclose a silver pair decked out with blood-red hearts. A large banner read 'Grand Third Year Sit-In' and sure enough kids were dropping to their bottoms by the score upon a good half centimetre of *frost*.

But half an hour later those same bottoms were seated sorrowfully once more on regulation steel frame chairs. The Grand Third Year Sit-In was at an end. Zena and Cindy were sitting in the Headmistress's room and Cindy's parents were on their way. (Not Mrs Wardle. She could not be traced.)

'I'm afraid this means suspension, Mr and Mrs Ashton,' said the Headmistress when they arrived, putting quivering fingertips not quite together.

Mrs Ashton broke into a wail. 'But this isn't our little girl,' she cried. She shot horrified glances in Cindy's direction. She saw time and again the nightmare vision of multi-layered multi-coloured leg-warmers above the shark's tooth hem of the regulation school skirt, bought at such expense and with all that Room for Growth. 'It isn't our little girl Cindy a-*tall*.' Both parents rose in their agitation, and the Headmistress rose as well. And Cindy rose too, tall as a hollyhock now her shoulders were straight and she held her flushed head so high. And Cindy Ashton looked down on them all, and she smiled.

6
MY COUSIN BROTHER

I wanted a bike more than anything else in the world. I kept dropping hints. It wasn't difficult for them to know what I wanted. It was my birthday two weeks ago. I couldn't get to sleep the night before, I was so excited. I had hinted and hinted, and I was sure this time I would get one. When I'd asked before, they'd pulled faces, but they *had* said, perhaps, when I was older. Well, I was older now, wasn't I? Surely fourteen was old enough.

I woke as soon as it was dawn and lay thinking about my bike. I didn't dare go downstairs and have a look because they'd be cross if I woke them up. We'd all gone to bed late the night before because my uncle had arrived from India. He was going to stay with us for a bit. He had one son with him. My cousin brother. He is called Vasan. The last thing I wanted in the world was another brother. I have one already. His name is Ashwin, and I hate him.

At last I heard the alarm go off in my parents' room. It seemed to be ages before they got up, though. But at long last I heard their bed give about a million creaks, and after a bit longer I heard my mother going downstairs. I counted up to a hundred, just to make it even more exciting, and then I put on my dressing-gown and went down.

'Happy birthday!' my mother said, and gave me a big kiss. I hugged her back, hardly daring to breathe, I was so excited. If I got dressed quickly and didn't bother with breakfast, I could have a ride before school. Even school wouldn't be too bad when I had a bike to ride as soon as I got home. I hate school.

'Your present is on the table in the front room,' said my mother gaily. 'I suppose you'll want to open it before you have your breakfast. I dare say there will be some more presents when everybody else gets up.'

But the thought of more couldn't make me feel any better. My blood had run cold when she said it was *on* the dining-room table and that I'd want to *open* it. It couldn't be a bike unless . . . Unless she was teasing me. Yes, of course, that was it. They *must* know what I wanted. They couldn't have failed to get the message. Mum was teasing me. Well, it was a good joke. I like a good laugh myself. Happily I ran through into the front room. And there was . . .

A big oblong parcel with a fat pink bow on it. I could have screamed. Slowly I walked towards it. I suppose it could just possibly be a not very expensive present, with the money for the bike inside. But I couldn't kid myself any longer. It was a big box. It wasn't a cheap present. Reluctantly I tore off the paper, and found . . .

A chemistry set! If there's one thing I detest at school more than school itself, it's any sort of Science. I'm hopeless at it.

Mum came in, beaming. 'You've opened it then,' she said. 'We thought it would help you at school. Your last report for Science was terrible, wasn't it? And you know how Dad likes you both to do well. Ashwin chose it for you – and, of course, he knows what he's doing. He got all As for Science on his first report, remember?' And Mum grinned enough to split her face at the thought of her brilliant little boy.

Remember? When was I ever allowed to forget? My parents never stop going on about Ashwin. How wonderful his first report at our school had been, what nice things the teachers had said about him at the Parents' Evening. It isn't fair. He was brought up in this country from nearly the beginning, speaking English. I had to learn to do *that* first, and I don't understand all the stuff they give us at school even now. But it's no good trying to tell them that. They say I'm making excuses for poor work. And anyway precious Ashwin's their *son*, isn't he? Their only *son*. So, of course, he's everything that's marvellous. It makes me sick. They've even promised they'll get him a bike, if his summer report's as good as his Christmas one. And he's only *eleven*.

At that moment Ashwin came charging into the room. 'It's magic, isn't it, Rash?' he said. 'Did Mum tell you I chose it? Here, let's open it up, and I'll show you what you can do with it.'

I couldn't bear it any longer. 'I'll tell you what you can do with it,' I screamed. 'You can stuff it. It's rubbish. I hate it.' And I tore from the room and rushed upstairs, screaming, before they could catch hold of me and stop me.

On the landing I saw my cousin brother Vasan standing in his pyjamas staring at me with his big round eyes. He'd come out of the room he was sharing with Ashwin to see what all the fuss was about, the creep.

'And you can get stuffed, too,' I hissed at him before I turned into my bedroom. 'I don't want any more *boys*!' I don't think he understood me. He doesn't speak much English. But I didn't care if I confused him. I rushed into my room and flung myself on to my bed, and cried and cried and cried . . .

That was the beginning of a very bad day – and it was my birthday! It's not fair, is it? Dad came up to my bedroom soon and told me off for being so ungrateful and for making such a noise. I had to go to school, of course. But I had cried so much that all my face was blotchy and swollen. I did look a sight. I was still crying a bit when I arrived at school, so I hung about the street until I heard the bell go so that the others couldn't see me. My cousin brother also had to go to school. It had all been arranged.

But Ashwin took him. He'd love that! Anybody to show off to!

Well, when I heard the bell go, I went into the yard, expecting to find the others lined up. But they were still running about. The teacher didn't come down for ages to blow the whistle. She must have forgotten to come on duty or something. They do sometimes forget. Trust it to happen just on the day when for once I *wanted* to go into school so that nobody could say anything about my blotchy face. I tried to keep to the edge of the playground so nobody could see me. I haven't any real friends. I told you, I don't really like school. But then somebody caught sight of me – and they can never leave anybody alone if they think there's something exciting, can they? Whenever I'd like someone to talk to me, nobody does, but that morning, when I wanted to be quiet on my own, a crowd of them came running up.

'Oh, look at Rashmiben,' said this really nasty girl called Melanie. 'What's the matter with her face? Ugh, I think she's got leprosy. Her cousin's come from India. Her brother told me this morning. I bet he's brought some disease with him. Don't go near her. You might catch something. Come away.' And they all ran off, screaming and shouting.

Thank goodness, the whistle went and we could go in. But they went on and on about me being diseased at Break. And after dinner they started again.

I wasn't going to stop there while they were all so horrible to me. Besides, I had started to cry again. I was going home. I'd never skived off before but I was going to now. The quickest way was through the boys' yard. I saw one girl who's all right, hanging about looking at me, but I wasn't going to stop. I didn't want anyone feeling sorry for me, thank you very much. I just wanted to go home.

I ran into the boys' yard where they were all shrieking and rushing about and fighting one another. I ran faster, hoping they wouldn't notice me.

Then suddenly I stopped dead. Directly in my path was my cousin brother, and he was crying too.

I didn't mean to, but I stopped to listen to what a crowd of first-year boys were yelling at him.

'Ape man, ape man!' they were shouting. 'Savage, savage!'

I saw Ashwin running around with his friends. For a moment he stopped and looked in a worried sort of way towards Vasan, but it was only for a moment. He was off again immediately, screaming and shouting with his precious white pals. Oh yes, Ashwin's dead popular with the pink ice-cream kids. He says it's because he knows so much General Knowledge and they all want him on their side when they have a Quiz, but I know it's because he's a creep and he buys loads of sweets and crisps and gives them to them. Anyway, here he was, supposed to be looking after our cousin brother, and he wouldn't do anything to stop him being bullied in case he fell out with his precious white mates. He makes me sick.

Vasan was really howling now. The other kids were laughing more than ever. Without thinking I rushed into the middle of them and grabbed Vasan out of reach of their jabbing fingers. I couldn't have turned on the girls for being horrible to me just now. Never in a million years. But I could get angry for Vasan. He hadn't done anything wrong and he was so little compared with that lot.

'What are you calling him names for?' I screamed at them. 'You're ignorant, you lot!'

The lads just laughed at me. Then the tallest of them spoke. 'He's a savage because he eats with his fingers,' he sneered at me. 'You should have seen him in the dining centre. He got a right telling-off from Sir. And he . . .' the boy creased up laughing, 'he burped dead loud at the end of dinner.' They all went off into screeches of laughter.

I felt very sorry for Vasan. I remember how difficult I had found it when I came to this country to learn to eat with a knife and fork. We eat our food with our fingers at home and use chapatis for mopping up our sauce. It's the Indian way. And I think it's much tidier than the way some of the white kids eat. They're always dropping stuff off their forks and eating off their knives and they shovel loads of food in all at once. I think it looks horrible. As for burping, well, in India it shows you're full. Anyway some of the white boys even burp in class. They do it on purpose and then say 'Pardon', and make everyone fall about.

The tall boy hadn't finished yet. 'And *that's* why he's an ape man.' He shrieked with delight. 'Just look at him now. He looks like a monkey with fleas.'

I looked at Vasan standing sobbing beside me, not understanding a word of what was going on. He was shivering with cold. There was a bitter wind and he was only wearing a thin jacket. All the other boys were wearing parkas with woolly linings. He had put his hands under his armpits to warm them, and his thin little face looked smaller than ever with the cold. He huddled his head deep down into the collar of his jacket. For a moment I saw him through the eyes of the others and I had to admit that he did look a bit like a monkey. A tiny baby one and very cold. I felt sorry for him. I seized his hand and began to run with him towards the gate. A loud jeer went up behind me and suddenly I heard Ashwin's voice shouting after me, sounding worried. Furious, I turned round. It was a bit late now for him to get involved. 'You lot are the savages,' I yelled as loud as I could. 'You as well, Ashwin.' And I turned and ran with Vasan and we didn't stop until we got out of the gate and down the road and round the corner.

I was in dreadful trouble when we reached home. I tried to explain how horrible the other kids had been to both of us, and also how Ashwin had done nothing to help, but would they listen? It couldn't be dear Ashwin's fault. They seemed to think that the fact that he was still there in school when we had come home was proof of this. I couldn't convince them. Vasan kept near to me all the time that they were going on at us. I was accused of leading him into bad ways. But he kept giving me these funny little smiles and following me about. They said it wasn't worth the fuss of getting us back into school that afternoon but we would have to go tomorrow properly or else . . . By the way, it was still my birthday, remember? Very funny, I don't think! What a birthday! I had told Vasan how I had wanted a bike when we were coming home from school. I had to talk to him in Gujerati, of course. He didn't say anything, but he nodded. I think he understood how I felt. He's not a bad kid. Piles better than Ashwin anyway.

I grew fed up with him hanging around me in the end. I had a lot of thinking to do and I needed to be on my own. I went up to my bedroom. I was fed up with school. I could never do well there like Ashwin. And that's all my parents want me to do – be a good student. And stick around at home and do the housework. Now the kids had started being horrible to me again, just like when I first came to this country. I couldn't bear it. And they hadn't given me a bike. This was the worst thing of all. Somehow I could have borne all the rest, if I'd just had a bike to escape on. I could have forgotten how much better at lessons Ashwin is than me and how they love him best. I could have forgotten the horrible things the other kids sometimes say. I would have been free when I came out of school. I could just have gone off somewhere on my own, with the wind tugging at my ears, and been free . . .

But here I was bikeless, bullied, bitter at my brother. Nobody loved me. Nobody cared how I felt. And the Science teacher had said we were going to have a test tomorrow and if you didn't get more than half marks you'd have the cane. Can they give girls the cane? I've never heard of it. Well, if I had to do that test, I'd know soon enough. I have never got anywhere near half marks in a Science test, and with leaving school at dinner time I hadn't taken my Science book home to revise . . .

At that moment the telephone rang. Of course, it had to be the Headmaster wanting to know if Vasan and I were at home, didn't it? Some dumb teacher had remembered I wasn't there at afternoon Registration and gone and asked Ashwin what had happened to me. Was I ill? And, of course, Grease-bag Ashwin had told on me, hadn't he? Said I'd taken off with Vasan and hadn't been seen since. My parents were full of apologies and said we'd both be in school tomorrow, they'd personally see to it. Nobody explained why we'd left school, of course . . . Ashwin wouldn't dare, because it would show him up as a coward. And my parents wouldn't take any notice of what I said. So everybody had decided we were just skivers. Typical, isn't it? Well, one thing was for certain. I wasn't going to school tomorrow. But how was I going to get out of it? I would have to make out I was ill, that was all.

But it would have to be something serious. I didn't intend going to school again in a long time. I'd rather go to hospital first.

Suddenly I had a brainwave. Mum complained sometimes of getting palpitations of the heart, and everybody got very steamed up about it. So when we were eating that night I suddenly let out a terrible groan, put my hand to my heart like I'd seen Mum do, and said my heart was beating jumpy and I felt breathless. But instead of leaping up and getting agitated the way they did with Mum, they all burst out laughing. Well, how was I to know I'd got the wrong side? I'm no better at Biology than I am at Chemistry. 'It must be indigestion,' said Know-all Ashwin. Dead original, I don't think. 'She bolts her food like a door.' And everybody went into fits again. I told you, I really hate my brother.

But I had had an idea. *Fits*, that was it. I'd pretend to have a fit. Then I'd lie stiff as anything and they'd think I was dead. They'd find out I wasn't soon enough, of course, but it would give them such a shock that they'd never think about sending me to school until they'd discovered what was wrong. Fits, yes. Now that should be good for a few weeks off . . .

I made up my mind not to start my fits until the next morning. There was less chance of them finding out that I was putting it on, the less time there was before going to school. So the next morning when my mother and Vasan were the only ones in the room, I suddenly threw myself on to the sofa with a terrible shriek and thrashed about a lot like I'd seen them do on telly, and then lay absolutely still and stiff with my eyes closed. Vasan gave a frightened cry and came pounding up to me. My mother came rushing up too. She never thought I was dead, though – I was most disappointed – but perhaps just lying stiff like that would frighten her nearly as much . . .

It certainly seemed to! Mum shrieked for Dad to come. I lay there stiff as stiff, my eyes tight shut. Dad came tearing in. He urgently said my name, very loud, and lightly touched my face with his fingers.

'It was kind of like a fit,' I heard Mum say in a frightened whisper. 'I'm sure there's something wrong with her, you know. She didn't seem well last night, did she? I know we laughed at her, but perhaps there really was something wrong. And she came home from school. She's never done that before.'

My dad grunted. 'Mmm, she could be having us on,' he said. 'I was sure she was faking last night, trying to get off school. Even so, I don't like the look of her now. Anyway, we've got to make sure. I'm going to ring for the doctor. Look how stiff she is.' He ran off to the hall to phone. Mum got down beside me and I felt her stroking my brow. I had to squeeze my fingers tight so as not to laugh. It tickled.

I was a bit worried when Dad said that about the doctor but I'd been expecting it. Would *he* know I was faking?

It seemed like ages before the doctor came. I was getting bored. Ashwin and Vasan had gone off to school. Dad works from home, so he kept coming in to have a look at me, or else Mum did, so I didn't dare open my eyes. I could tell which one was with me by the sound of their footsteps.

Suddenly there was a commotion at the front door. I thought it was the doctor and I squeezed my hands shut even tighter. But then I heard them shouting, my uncle's voice louder than any other, and I realized that Vasan had come home from school again. The kids must have been bullying him in the yard. They were really cross with him, and I heard him start to bawl. Why hadn't Ashwin taken care of him? He might have known they'd start again. They can never resist it when somebody's frightened of them. I heard the grown-ups telling him that he'd have to go back. But then there was a ring on the doorbell and it was the doctor. Vasan was forgotten in the agitation.

I lay stiffer than ever. I heard them all come into the room and a dark shadow fell across me. I knew the doctor was leaning over me. I kept really still. Suddenly he pulled up one of my eyelids. I nearly screamed but I'd been lying stiff for so long now that I managed to keep a grip on myself by clenching my fingers hard. All the same I'm sure I jumped. Do people having a fit ever jump?

'It's like she's paralysed,' I heard Dad say in a frightened whisper.

'Mmm, it's nothing like that,' said the doctor rather sternly. 'It's a hysterical reaction to something.' He must have seen that my parents didn't understand him. I didn't understand him either. When he said, 'It's nothing like that', I thought he knew I was faking. Now *I* was worried. It sounded as if there really *was* something wrong with me.

The doctor went on to explain to my parents. They must have been looking very confused.

'It's all in her mind,' he said at last. 'Will you excuse me if I make a phone call?'

My parents said that was all right, sounding very shocked, and I heard Dad telling him where the phone was. He went out to show him. I lay there, *really* stiff now, from terror! In the mind! That meant he thought I'd gone mad! Who was he telephoning? Was he going to take me away to some loony bin? I began to feel very uncomfortable indeed!

I heard my dad come back in the room and shut the door. Then I heard the worried voices of my dad, my mum and my uncle.

'This is a terrible thing indeed,' my dad said. 'It sounds as if he thinks she really has gone crazy.'

My mum gave a gasp and a little cry. 'You know what this will mean, don't you? They'll take her away, and even if she is all right, all the neighbours will find out. No one will want to have anything to do with our family any more. They will never allow any of their sons to marry her. No one will want to marry any of our children. They will be too afraid of the madness. Oh, I can't believe it! My little daughter – mad!' and she started to cry loudly. I listened, horrified.

'What can have caused this terrible thing to happen?' I heard my mother say in a choked voice after a moment. 'Can . . . can it be a spirit? She told me not so long ago that she'd seen that old woman down the road – you know, who died – standing in her room. I told her it was only a dream. But who knows?'

'She certainly seems very sick,' my uncle agreed in a mournful sort of voice.

Suddenly I heard a kind of howl of rage. It was Vasan! I'd forgotten he was there.

'*You're* the ones who are sick,' he shouted. 'You are the ones who are ill in your minds. You don't listen to her, do you? She told you what it's like at that school. And she's right. It's horrible there. I hate it and I'm never going again. I'm not. I'm not. I bet she never wants to go again. I bet that's why she's got sick. And you didn't give her a bike. You didn't, and she said you knew how much she wanted one. She said it and said it, but you didn't listen. You only listen to what you want to hear. Like Ashwin.

You always believe what he says. You said he was to take care of me but he didn't. He doesn't care. Rashmiben looked after me. She cares. She's nice. But you're going to buy *Ashwin* a bike. It's not fair. You've *made* her be sick. And Ashwin hit me today, with the others. I hate him, and I want to go home. OW!'

At the end I heard my uncle slap him across the face, a sharp slap like a gun going off.

I leapt up from the sofa. 'Stop it, stop it!' I screamed, and at that moment the doctor came back into the room . . .

I thought we'd both get into terrible trouble, but that doctor was really nice. He asked my parents if he could talk to me on my own and he asked me lots of questions and I told him the whole story – you know, very much the story I've decided to write down here today. He said it's a good idea to write things down that upset you. Well, I'm not upset any more, but I *was* upset, wasn't I? And I thought I'd have a bit of practice in case I ever get upset again. Anyway, I think it's great writing stories. I've never written a huge long one like this before. Isn't it long? But come to think of it, I've always liked writing stories at school and the English teacher once said that one was quite good. That was in the first year. Perhaps I'll show her this one sometime. I bet she won't be able to believe that I could write a great long one like this. It'll take her ages to read it.

Come to think of it, I don't really mind English so much at school. It's not bad. Anyway, I don't mind school so much any more. Not now that . . . But I'm jumping ahead of myself. The doctor wanted a long chat with my parents and they wouldn't let me hear. I wonder what they said? They didn't tell me.

But they didn't put me in a loony bin. And the

neighbours never found out. And Vasan and I didn't get in any more trouble! Amazing! I thought we would but we didn't. Even though they found out I was faking. And he'd been skiving, of course.

And now here is the happy ending. I like stories with happy endings, don't you? On the next Saturday morning when I came down for breakfast my mother was grinning again.

'Go into the front room first,' she said.

'Why?' I asked, but she wouldn't say. I looked surprised. I wandered in and there was . . .

Yes, you've guessed it . . . a *bike*! I sat on it and stroked it and even cried for a moment. Then I rushed off to hug her. It was exactly the kind I wanted. I wonder how they knew? Dad came in, grinning too. 'I think you might give that chemistry set to Ashwin and Vasan, don't you?' he said. 'You don't seem to be getting much use out of it.'

I grinned back. 'That sounds like a great idea,' I said.

But do you know, once the lads got playing with it, making bangs and smells and different colours, I got quite interested and I even joined in with them, even though they are only little boys. And it was quite good fun, I was surprised.

I've been very busy since then with my bike and telling this story. I didn't know what to call it. 'The Bike' doesn't sound quite right. You'd know that I'd get one in the end if I called it that. So I thought I'd dedicate it to my cousin brother. He sort of comes into it, doesn't he? He's friendly with Ashwin these days. In fact, they're mates now. I let them get on with it. They're not good for much, boys, are they?

Although there's quite a nice boy in our class, come to think of it. I see him when I'm out and about. On my bike . . .

7
THE BATTLE OF
THE MANDAS

Amanda Heyward and Amanda Green were best mates. They sat together in Registration. They sat together in class. They sat together on the swimming bus and on the wall by the bus stop. But it was only on the wall by the bus stop that they ever *stayed* sitting together. Everywhere else there was some teacher waiting to get them, then to fling them to opposite poles of the globe.

It was Miss Moore, the R.I. teacher, who called them the two Mandas. 'Manda Heyward,' she would say, 'was that you flicking laggy bands at Manda Green?'

'No-o, Miss!'

'Of course it was. I thought I told you two never to sit together in my lesson again. *Move*, Manda Heyward, and *sharp*!'

'Aw, Miss. But listen, Miss . . .'

Miss Moore would hold up a palm. '*Don't* attempt to explain. Just take up thy bed and *walk*.'

'But I haven't got a *bed*, Miss. So I don't *really* have to move, Miss, do I, Miss?' And Manda Heyward would tilt her head on to her shoulder and open her eyes very wide.

But Miss Moore didn't flinch from fixing Manda Heyward with *her* eyes, very terribly, and pointing towards the far left-hand back corner like some Old Testament prophet of doom. And Amanda Heyward would slouch across the classroom and fling herself on to a chair, half turning her back to the rest of the class and muttering away.

Usually when this happened she'd start scribbling a note. On the day that the battle of the Mandas was declared, this is what it said:

To Amanda 'Rentamouth' Green. Pass It On.
Did you know that Denise wants to go out with Pete Tebbit? I asked him if he'd go out with Denise.

Very soon the note was on its way back to sender, with additions. This is how it read:

> To Amanda 'Slagheap' Heyward. Pass It On.
> (1) What did he say?
> (2) Does Denise know?

Another addition was made:

> To Amanda 'Fat Face' Green. By Special Delivery.
> Denise does know because we saw Pete down the chippy and he said he didn't know because he wants to go out with Karen *and* Denise.

Amanda Green's note came back:

> To Amanda 'Toe Rag' Heyward. By Registered Post.
> Yes, BUT (1) Denise told me she wouldn't go out with him now if you paid her
> BUT (2) I bet she would if he asked her
> AND (3) Do you want to go out with any lad yourself?

Amanda Heyward was so agitated when she received this note that she couldn't wait for her reply to jerk its way back to Amanda Green by a series of nudges. So she stood, lined up her shot and threw while Miss Moore was otherwise engaged.

> To Amanda 'The Slug' Green. By Air.
> (1) and (2) Yes, I know she would but she tells everybody she wouldn't because she only told me that she would. But don't tell her I told you.
> (3) NO!!!!!!!!!!!!!!!!!!!!!!!!!!!!!!!!
> (4) DO YOU?

The return note dive-bombed on to Amanda Heyward's desk from quite a height and with some degree of violence:

To Amanda 'The Dog' Heyward. By Carrier Pigeon.
(1) NOT LOIKELY!!!!!!!!!!!!!!!!!!!!!!!!
(2) Bog off!!!!!!!!!!!!!

But both Mandas were remembering what had happened in netball that morning. And each Manda knew that the other Manda lied through her teeth . . .

The two Mandas were ace at sport. They were in the second-year netball team and Mr Kirby's mixed basketball. In netball Amanda Heyward played defence. She was tall and thin with long pale hair and a long pale face. Amanda Green played attack and was short and dark with curls and specs, sturdy legs and a lot of go. You could imagine Amanda Green not looking all that much different at forty, in something low-cut behind a bar, wearing specs inlaid with jewels and being very good for custom. Basketball was the two Mandas' best sport and Mr Kirby was their best teacher, Mrs Mackay who took them for netball, their worst.

Mrs Mackay was fierce and fair and fifty. She had high standards and wasn't easily impressed. Those who liked her worshipped her. Those who didn't didn't.

'Amanda Green, those plimsolls are a Disgrace. Hair *back*, Amanda Heyward.'

'Aw, Mi-iss. Miss, if it carries on *freezing* like this, can we wear our track-suits for the match on Sat'day?'

'Indeed no. The standard of a team is set by the standard of its dress. A navy skirt and a *white* blouse, Amanda Green, is what the school uniform states, and so it shall remain.'

'We can play basketball in whatever we like. T'ain't fair!'

Mrs Mackay shuddered. 'The word "basketball", Amanda Heyward, is as Discord in my ears. I am about to

have Words with Mr Kirby and the Headmaster on the
whole subject of girls' basketball. It is the *ruination* of your
netball skills. All very well for you to opt for it further up
the school *if* you so must.' Mrs Mackay showed with a
sniff the standard of any girl who opted for basketball
further up.

'Basketball any day,' muttered Amanda Heyward. 'No
way I'd take netball further up. *No way*.'

'Mr Kirby's a laugh,' muttered Amanda Green. 'All you
get with netball is nag, nag, nag.'

'What's that you're saying, Amanda Green?' demanded
Mrs Mackay. 'If it's worth spending the breath, it's worth
sharing the toil.'

'Nothing, Miss,' replied Amanda Green, smiling
sweetly. She turned slowly in the direction of Amanda
Heyward, the smile fixed on her face, and mimed being
sick.

At that moment Ian Linthwaite started across the yard
carrying a very large sheet of black card. It was nearly as
large as Ian Linthwaite. All the two Mandas could see were
Ian Linthwaite's legs, but they knew it was him on account
of the brothel-creepers. Only Ian Linthwaite could get away
with five inches of crêpe sole. 'Wanna look at me skeling-
ton, Miss?' Ian asked Mrs Mackay good-naturedly. 'I'm off
to show it the 'Ead.' He jerked the card round so that they
could see the other side which was all over white paper
bones, cut out to resemble the de-fleshed human form.
They also saw for a second that the brothel-creepers
extended upwards into an entire Ted suit that belonged to
Ian's dad – tapered trousers, bootlace tie, long jacket, the
lot. Then as Mrs Mackay gasped an outraged 'Well!' Ian
Linthwaite took off, gliding along on his cushion of crêpe
like a playing card of Death.

And both Mandas looked like they'd been dealt the joker in the pack. For as they caught sight of the Ted suit and the long wedge of hair that fell across one eye and the lazy way Ian's head nodded on his shoulders as if not quite firmly attached, they both saw how *fanciable* Ian Linthwaite had become, transformed in the twinkling of a card to frog prince from pimply scruff.

And each Manda saw that the other Manda saw. And though one played defence and the other attack *for the same team* they managed to crash into one another forehead on, as fierce as a couple of spring rams in pursuit of a favourite ewe . . .

Back in R.I. Miss Moore had problems of her own. Miss Moore had more kids excused her lesson on religious grounds than she had kids taking the lesson. The first fifteen minutes were spent in going through the excuse notes and in heated debate.

It was the turn of Pete Tebbit to produce one today. 'Dear Miss Moore,' it read. 'My son must not do R.I. as he is Church of England. Yours sincerely, Mrs R.I.P. Tebbit (mother of Pete.)'

Miss Moore was past arguing. Miss Moore was past caring. She waved Pete to a corner of the room where those excused R.I. went in for private study. That is to say, they talked, drew, talked, read comics, talked, played noughts and crosses and generally distracted the others. Pete Tebbit ended up in the same corner as Amanda Heyward.

'How about Denise?' she hissed.

Pete looked her up and down. He hitched his neck to one side of his collar and then to the other, straightened his jacket on the shoulders by tugging on his lapels and swelled. 'Denise ain't *bad*,' he said. 'But Karen ain't either. Come to think of it, you ain't bad yourself.' He flashed her a greasy leer and leaned across her to pick up one of the work sheets Miss Moore left in the window-sills for when you'd completed your Task of the Day. He flicked through it, then looked more closely and gasped. He charged with it up to the front. 'Miss. Hey, Miss. Look at this, Miss.'

Miss Moore pursed her lips. 'I don't think you ought to be looking at those, Peter, do you? Bearing in mind that you are Church of England and as such excused R.I.' Miss Moore quivered a little with distress.

'Oh, Mi–iss. Go on, Miss.'

'I think not, Peter. It's against your mother's principles and as such would not be right.'

'Oh, *yeah*, Miss. Go on. You've *got* to tell me why they're drowning this baby.'

Miss Moore looked at Peter with despair. 'They are not *drowning* it, Peter. They are *baptizing* it.'

There was a great pounding on the door. Ian Linthwaite, come to announce the arrival in school of the Nit Nurse. Ian Linthwaite was no good at lessons but turned nasty if anyone pointed this out. So he spent most of his time in the art block, only emerging to treat the Headmaster to a private view of his latest masterpiece or to run errands for the Deputy Head. In such innocent ways Ian Linthwaite passed over time that might otherwise have been spent in blowing up the school.

'Lads first,' said Ian Linthwaite, weight on one hip, passing a hand heavy with responsibility across his wedge of forehead hair. Amanda Green and Amanda Heyward both let out a sigh, then swung towards one another and glared.

'Line up then, boys,' said Miss Moore, resigned to the loss of the rest of her lesson. 'Wait *quietly* outside the medical room door. We don't want the complaints from Nurse we had last time.'

The girls were hushed when the boys had gone. Many placed hands thoughtfully on the tops of their heads and scratched. Manda Heyward and Manda Green, who usually combed through one another's scalps with their fingers like two affectionate chimps, continued to glare.

Miss Moore caught wind of the glare. 'The girls can go in *two* groups,' she announced firmly. 'Go ahead, Manda Heyward. Wait on, Manda Green.'

The boys came screaming back from the Nit Nurse in ones and twos. They were always extremely loud when relieved. Unfortunately they'd been extremely loud right across the yard, through the cloakroom and into the main building, and the Deputy Head had heard. So the girls were sent back in their two separate blocks, first Manda Heyward's and ten minutes later Manda Green's. Ian Linthwaite escorted back both groups of girls. When Manda Green arrived, she posed in the doorway, one hand on a hip, one hip at an angle, one hand in the air and limp from the wrist, both eyes on Ian Linthwaite and said, 'Well, gang, Manda Heyward's got nits.'

Ian Linthwaite started to grin, but Manda Heyward leapt like an antelope and snatched at Manda Green's curls. Manda Green got her head down and charged for Manda Heyward's stomach. Manda Heyward put her knee up and winded Manda Green as she charged. Manda Green fell forward and seized Manda Heyward's knees as she fell. Manda Heyward toppled over, falling across Manda Green's back as she toppled. Manda Green reared up and Manda Heyward landed on her nose as she reared. Manda Heyward shoved her bottom up and Manda Green pitched forward as she shoved. Manda Green crash-landed on her forehead and then they both thrashed about a good deal, punching, kicking, scratching, wrestling, screaming, pinning down arms, pinning down legs, knees in throats, teeth in knees, and generally carrying on. Ian Linthwaite watched in delight, then made for a jug of near-dead chrysanths. He lined up the jug, then chucked and the two Mandas rose up like water goblins, quivering, shrieking, and trailing green slime.

It was Denise who explained it was all because they wanted to go out with Ian Linthwaite. She explained this in front of the entire class and Ian Linthwaite, not to mention Miss Moore. 'Well, Amanda Green certainly ain't bad,' said Pete Tebbit thoughtfully, forgetful that he had made the same claim for Amanda Heyward that very afternoon. Denise glared at him and went looking for Ian Linthwaite after school to find out what he was going to do about the Mandas.

'Mr Kirby's having a second-year disco,' Ian Linthwaite said after thought, 'in the dinner hour, Wednesday. I'll decide which one then.' Denise passed on the message.

The Deputy Head, who did not approve of dinner-time discos, said it had to be strict school uniform or else. But Amanda Heyward wound her lemon hair round into a top-knot and wound the top-knot round with a bit of tinsel with some sky blue swansdown attached. And Amanda Green took one look at her in the cloakroom mirror and took herself off to the Art block, found some lime-green paint and gave herself some very fine streaks. At the disco Ian Linthwaite looked at the lime-green paint and at the sky-blue swansdown and back at the lime-green paint and chose the swansdown in spite of the threat of nits. He didn't dance with Manda Heyward *much*, though, preferring to do a sort of creeping crawling solo dance of his own. In the

Ted suit and crêpe soles he drew quite a crowd as he buckled himself about, singing 'See the Little Robin Go Tweet Tweet Tweet' to a funky version of 'Rockin' Robin'. But he did leave the gym with his arm round Manda Heyward.

The next day that same arm crept round Manda Green. And the next, round Manda Heyward. And so on.

Both Mandas complained a great deal to Denise. 'Why not have another scrap?' suggested Denise who had relished the last one. But both Mandas recalled the swollen eyes, the thick lips, the sore ribs and green slime, and thought not.

'Well, you play opposite sides in mixed basketball, don't you?' recalled Denise. 'The next match could be a fight to the death.' Denise rubbed her hands and the two Mandas declared it an ace scheme.

Denise carried the news to Ian Linthwaite. Monday lunchtime he turned up in the gym. So did Pete Tebbit, Denise and the rest of their class. Manda Heyward rushed up and presented Ian with a red paper rose off a cracker before the match began. And Manda Green's favour was a pale blue silk handkerchief on loan from her dad.

Mr Kirby threw the ball up, Manda Heyward got her fingers to it and the reds had possession. Andrew Plummet pounded it down the gym, pivoted, bouncing it from hand to hand, accelerated and tossed it to Manda Heyward, who leapt, hung in the air and scored. The crowd bayed and Manda Green scowled.

But the blues had possession. John Baker dribbled, pointed, shouted instructions and flipped the ball to Manda Green, who circled out of harm's way, spurted and rose up like water – the perfect jump shot. A klaxon sounded, feet drummed, Amanda Heyward scowled.

But Manda Heyward had the ball. Manda Green, though, was the finest guard Mr Kirby's mixed basketball had yet known (so said Mr Kirby) and she sparked forward like a jumping jack, cheekily patting the ball from under Manda Heyward's long fingers. But Manda Heyward was upon her and stuck out a crafty elbow as she shot. Mr Kirby blasted on the whistle, signalling like a tic-tac man – intentional foul.

Manda Heyward bounced the ball nearly to the ceiling in pique. Manda Green looked sideways at Ian Linthwaite and wiped her palms on her skirt. She shuffled till the ground and her feet felt as one. Then she took a deep breath and launched her shot. It fell clean through the net. Mr Kirby held up two fingers. Manda Green squared up again. A crescendo of foot stomping from the reds, but the ball soared and fell once again, true and sweet.

Manda Green was now on the defensive, arms out-stretched like a kid on a tightrope, neck jerking like an agitated hen's, eyes spinning in all directions like pinballs. But Manda Heyward had the ball and her legs scissored in the air as she shot. And scored.

The score flapped backwards and forwards after that like swing doors. Two minutes before the end Pete Tebbit called a 'time out' – for both teams at once! Denise ran on to the floor to mop up the sweat. Both Mandas watched Pete spellbound as he psyched up *both* teams. 'C'mon, the Blues. C'mon, you Reds. Let's go, let's go.' But it was Manda Green who spurted, gained possession, dodged, penetrated, twisted as she jumped and scored.

The crowd were on their feet. Those feet stamped. Klaxons wailed. The blues had their arms out now, heads twitching like Indian dancers. They mopped and they mowed. They leapt and they dived. They patted at the ball. And when the final whistle went Manda Green turned in triumph to lay hands on her prize.

But Ian Linthwaite had gone. The chair that they had draped with a furry bath mat to look like a throne was empty. Only Pete Tebbit stood behind it, looking glum.

'Wh . . . where's he gone?' gasped both Mandas.

'Off,' mourned Pete Tebbit, 'with Denise.'

That afternoon the two Mandas sat together once more. They didn't *stay* sitting together, of course, but on the wall by the bus stop there they were, side by side.

'He's made a monkey out of us,' said Manda Heyward. 'Tell you what, we'll both go out with another lad each and have us revenge. And swear never ever to go out with that greasy creep again, I don't care *how* much he begs.'

So they went to Manda Heyward's together and there in the garden shed nicked their thumbs and mixed blood in true sisterhood.

'Decided who you fancy going out with yet?' Manda Heyward casually asked her mate Manda Green.

Manda Green smiled as she nodded. There was a picture in her mind.

'How 'bout you?'

Manda Heyward nodded too, seeing a picture as she smirked.

And if you could have taken the lids off their heads like two teapots, you'd have seen Pete Tebbit crouching there, ordering each to take a 'time-out' and urging her with love, 'C'*mon*, Manda. Atcha girl, Manda. Let's go, let's go!'

8
THE RAINBOW CLOCK

'Dear Delroy,' wrote Surinder. 'How are you? I hope you are doing well in school.'

Surinder stared in front of him at the objects on his desk top. His dad had bought him the desk only this year, so that he could study in his bedroom. That's what he ought to be doing, studying, not struggling with a letter to blooming Delroy. Surinder began to arrange his biros and pencils in a neat line along the desk top, and straightened every book and every piece of paper. Then he took the pencils out of the straight line and sharpened every one. With a sigh he returned at last to the letter. He read through what he had written five times, and stared in front of him again.

Surinder hated writing letters. He hated it at any time, but tonight there were so many other things he ought to be doing. There was his Biology homework for a start. Then he wanted to revise Chemistry for half an hour and work on some Physics problems for another half and then read the paper for fifteen minutes (so important to keep up with World Events). He looked in despair at the three pages of closely packed writing that his friend from Birmingham had sent and he sighed. Hadn't Delroy anything better to do these days? When they'd lived next door to one another before Surinder had moved to Leicester, they used to spend every evening together, studying. They'd done projects together. They'd tested one another when it came to exams. They'd built kits together when Surinder's timetable said 'Half an Hour's Necessary Relaxation Time'. Delroy had even copied Surinder's timetable, so that when it was 9.55 p.m., 'Time for a Relaxing Drink and Fifteen Minutes with Newspaper And/Or First Half of "News at Ten" ', Surinder knew that next door Delroy would know it was time for exactly the same thing.

Now Delroy had time on his hands, it seemed, to squander writing a whole lot of rubbish about *girls*! Surinder snorted.

He got up and drew his bedroom curtains together so that they lined up exactly and sat down again and took up his pen. He was the only person he knew to use proper ink and a fountain pen, just like his father had before him. He carefully drew a hair out of the nib and wiped his fingers on a tissue from the box he had covered with computer paper and labelled TISSUES in bold black ink. He was proud of that touch. 'Something a little bit *different*,' he had said to Delroy when he came to stay. Delroy had thought his room was great. Everything in it was black and white – black and white graph-paper curtains, a white Anglepoise lamp on his black fibreglass desk, filing cabinet white with black handles, black and white chess set cover on his bed, black and white digital clock on the white table by the bedside. Only the carpet was beige – white would have got filthy, black would have shown up the bits. Surinder hated bits. There were no unnecessary objects on Surinder's shiny surfaces, no pictures on his gleaming white walls. 'Wish my dad had the bread to let me kit out my room like this,' Delroy had said to Surinder, running his brown hands with their pale pink nails admiringly over the lacquered veneers, clean as an operating theatre. He eyed again the tissue box neatly backed with computer paper and labelled TISSUES in bold black ink.

But the fact that Delroy might even now also be drawing a white tissue from a tissue box wrapped in computer paper and labelled TISSUES in bold black ink was no comfort to Surinder. Delroy was a dead loss these days, a waste of precious time.

'I am sorry I couldn't write this letter earlier on, as I am revising for the Christmas exams.' Surinder stuck his tongue down his pen top and whistled dolefully, pulling at his turban. He'd never be done at this rate. One sentence every five minutes. Surinder thought again.

'Will you write me at the most once a month, not once a week, as it is more economical.' Surinder looked at his watch: 7.41. His timetable said, '7.55: *If time*, go downstairs for Reviving Cup of Coffee'. There was no way he could take fifteen minutes just getting down the stairs. Perhaps he could squeeze in fifteen minutes of *The Times* and catching up with World Events? Or fifteen minutes 'Exercising Time: A Healthy Mind in a Healthy Body'? No, he'd only have twelve minutes and forty-three seconds at it now. Surinder shuddered. That wouldn't do at all. But twelve minutes and thirty-odd seconds struggling to write to his friend!

'I always find it hard to write letters as I don't know what to say. If English was my best subject, not my worst, I would find it easy. As you know, my best subject is Physics, next is Chemistry.' Inspiration at last! 'Talking about writing, you remember that white fellow Robert Russell (Rusty) you met when you were here? His ambition is to be 'aerodynamic engineer' yet he dosen't do any homework. For instance, Afzal was away for a week and I borrowed him all my school books so he could catch up. It took him just one night to catch everything up. Some time ago Robert missed 3½ days off school and he still hasen't caught up with the average pupils despite me and Afzal borrowing him our books *many times*.'

Surinder, encouraged by this flood, thought again.

'You remember that fellow Salim I used to write you

about? Well I do not hang around with Salim so much now as he is usually absent.

'With best wishes.

Yours sincerely,

Surinder Singh (Mr)

146 Upton Street,

Leicester,

LE2 4PG

Great Britain,

United Kingdom,

The Free World.'

'P.S. Tommorow is our first EXAM.'

Surinder looked at his watch. He leapt up, folded the paper so that the two edges met precisely, slid it into the envelope, flicked with his tongue to the right, to the left, and stuck the letter down with a bang of the fist. He took the stairs two at a time and made it to the kettle just as the digital clock flickered to 7.55 . . .

It was a week later and Surinder was struggling with composition again. In his English lesson this time. The exams were over, and they were back to routine with double English. Bor-ing.

They'd just done Duncan being murdered by Macbeth. 'I want you to make up your own newspaper,' said Mr Melbourne. 'The main story will be the murder of Duncan. Splash headlines. King slain at Thane of Cawdor's castle. You know the kind of thing. Exclusive interview with Lady Macbeth. Report on the foulness of the night. Feature on local superstitions – horses eating one another. That sort of thing. Then anything you like to make it lively – puzzles, adverts, sports reports, cartoons, special interest stories. Just use your imagination.'

Surinder groaned. A whole double period to be filled with all that *writing*! 'Anything you like,' he said. 'Just use your imagination,' he said. Well, Surinder simply hadn't *got* an imagination. And that was that.

When the bell rang at the end of the first lesson, Surinder had written at the top of his large sheet of paper, 'The Scottish Times'. Underneath he had written, 'King Slain at Thane of Cawdor's Castle'. Underneath *that* he had written, 'The king was slain last night at the Thane of Cawdor's castle. There is an exclusive interview with Lady Macbeth on page two. The weather was fowl. The horses ate one another. Inside you will find puzzles, adverts, sports reports and special interest stories.'

After that he'd been pulling at his turban and getting ink on his tongue from sticking it down his pen top and making very discreet popping noises. Surinder looked around at what the other kids were doing. Afzal was staring out of the window. Very very occasionally he'd make a mark on a piece of paper. He was counting how many BMWs went past the school in a week. Afzal meant to own a BMW by the time he was thirty. If too many went past, though, he'd change it to a Lotus Élite.

David March was staring at the ceiling where a spider promenaded round and round the rim of the light just above his desk. Every now and then the spider would burn its feet and spin a hasty web. But it always climbed up to the same light bowl again. Surinder sighed.

Wasn't *anybody* working properly? Surinder's eye fell on Topaz Smith. She had her head down and was scribbling frantically with a pale pink plastic ballpoint shaped to look like a quill pen. Every now and then her shoulders would heave up and down.

Topaz Smith was a weirdo. She was always in trouble for

her multi-coloured patchwork jackets, her floating scarves and her dingle-dangle ear-rings. She had a spiky red fringe and a streaky pony-tail growing out of one ear and went on and on in Discussion. Topaz Smith did not know her place and Surinder couldn't stand her.

Topaz dashed down the quill pen and snatched up a pencil. (She did everything in fits and starts.) She examined the end of it with a grand gesture, flung her fingers against the spiked fringe and groaned. Then she tore across to the waste-paper basket where she was soon joking with Candy Atkinson. Sir let them talk while they worked if they wanted to, which Surinder thought a grave mistake.

Cautiously Surinder left his desk and bent over Topaz's paper to see what all the scribbling was about.

Topaz had called her newspaper 'The Daily Rain'. She had drawn a huge puddle in the top left-hand corner with a giant raindrop plopping into it. 'Read "The Daily Rain",' it said, 'for the best in Splash Headlines.' Surinder snorted. Trust it to be silly! The front page was dominated by a single word picked out in vivid tartan. 'MACDEATH!' it read. 'By your raving reporter Jock Strapp.' The report began: 'It was Macduff who first beheld the gherrizzly, gherrastly, gherrimish sight. "There was only one word for it," Macduff was quoted as saying, "MACabre." ' Surinder snorted again, quickly scanning the headlines of the other news items:

HAGGIS WORKERS SAY 'NO' TO SOYA BEAN

LEYLAND CARTS GO ON STRIKE

STUPID BOY TO LIVE ON PIG FARM

And the advertisements:

'Bill's kilts: With sporran. Complete satisfaction
guaranteed.
Send large carrier pigeon to . . .'
'Coffinmate. Coffee for Vampires.'
'Protect your sporran from MOTH.'
'Personal. Small dog requires large cat for
chasing round garden and
GENUINE FRIENDSHIP.'

Surinder looked at the Special Features. 'Exclusive interview with Society Hostess, Lady "Chi Chi" Macbeth. Page Three.' Surinder turned over the page. A cut-out picture of Joan Collins, showing a lot of cleavage and raising a Martini glass, winked up at him. Surinder closed his eyes. When he opened them again his attention was caught by something in the Sports Report.

SEMI-FINAL OF SPLENDID MACJOUST
Sir Hamish versus Sir Beamish.
Sir Angus versus Surinder.
Favourite to Win: Surinder Singer Sewing Machine. Six
to Four On.

Surinder's mouth twitched at the same time as his eyebrows knitted. For his name was entirely surrounded with hearts! He turned over the page and caught his breath again. For there was a huge picture of a very large turban, a maroon turban, *his* turban, upside down with a load of rubbish spewing out of it. And across it, so there could be no doubt, Topaz had scrawled 'TUR-BIN'. Underneath she had written, 'Top Quality Refuse Depository: SURIN'S TUR-BINS'. In spite of the insult, though, the SURIN was still surrounded by hearts!

At that moment Topaz bounded back. Surinder quickly flapped the page over.

'What you doing round my desk, Surinder?' demanded Topaz. There was a hopeful look in her eyes.

Surinder was caught off his guard. He couldn't tackle her there and then about the dread insult she'd paid him. Besides, he recalled Surinder, Favourite to Win, and the hearts, and he didn't know quite what to think!

'I . . . I wondered if I could look at your Macbeth book,' Surinder said feebly, 'to get some ideas.' Topaz had her own copy of the play, new out. Her mum had brought it back for her, a present from London. Sir had shown them all. It was the real play but all done in cartoons. Sir thought it was great, Surinder that it was daft.

'Forgot it today,' said Topaz, crossing her fingers and edging her bag out of sight with her toe. 'But you can come round my house after school and borrow it, Surinder. Stay to tea if you like.'

Surinder could not believe his ears. Go to a *girl's* house? She had to be out of her mind. 'S'all right,' he said. 'Got too much work to do. Haven't the time.'

'I'll bring it round your house after tea then,' said Topaz straight off, looking at him with the bright eyes of a spider who has just netted a particularly dense fly. With a heavy heart Surinder settled back down to attempt another headline story. 'HAGGIS WORKERS SAY "NO" TO SOYA BEAN . . .'

So quarter to four witnessed the unlikely sight of Surinder Singh walking home with Topaz Smith. 'Can't stop,' muttered Surinder, eyes dodging this way and that. 'Haven't the time. I'll just pick the book up, then go.'

Topaz looked at him. She scrabbled in her peacock-tail-shaped shoulder bag and drew out a cartoon she'd done. It showed an alarm clock with a long grey beard, wearing a crown and a kilt, with a dagger up its nose and sitting in a puddle of blood. Underneath it said, 'Macbeth hath murdered Time.' She handed it to him. 'There you are, Surinder,' she said. 'Time's dead. You needn't worry about Time any longer.' Surinder looked at it and looked at her. He was at a complete loss. 'It's *sleep*,' he said scornfully at last. 'Macbeth hath murdered *sleep*.' Topaz stared at him. Then with a shake of her head and a heave of her shoulders she pulled out her plastic quill, took the cartoon from him, stopped at a wall, leant the paper on it and drew the alarm clock, some closed eyes and a lot of trailing ZZZZZZZZZZZZZZZZs coming out of his bloody nose, and changed *Time* to *Sleep*. She put the pen and the cartoon away and bounded very close to Surinder. 'You're a slave to your brain, you know that, Sewing Machine?' she said affectionately, jogging up against his elbow. 'And *nearly* as boring as Afzal.'

Topaz stopped by the front gate of a terraced house in Norland Street. To say it was a terraced house doesn't make it sound very exciting. Surinder lived in a terraced house very similar to this one. That is to say, the same structure, the same stone scrolls on either side of the door, the same mangy-looking privet hedge round the tiny paved front garden. But whereas Surinder's house was a discreet fume-blackened stone with discreet smut-ingrained stone scrolls, and discreetly painted with the dark green paint that had become regulation for that block, Topaz's house was more like a child's idea of a house, entirely constructed of sweets. The front door was barley-sugar gold; the left-hand downstairs window frames were a lollipop red and the right a peppermint green, while upstairs they were sherbet lemon and blackcurrant purple; the entire facing wall was painted milk chocolate, with one scroll the jewel colours of wine-gums, and the other, sugar-almond shades – soft pink, peach and the palest of aquamarines. Topaz's house looked good enough to eat.

Except you didn't eat houses. Houses, like schools, meant good solid achievement, the sound investment of time. Surinder sniffed.

Topaz opened the door. It wasn't locked. Instead of going into a dark narrow hall with the stairs leading steeply out, you stepped into a big room with the stairs going out of one corner. The Smiths had knocked down a wall. You could tell they had knocked it down because they had left bits of it lying untidily about.

The room was like a puppet theatre hit by the blitz. The walls that still stood were painted a fiery orange, the wall up the stairs was purple and the floorboards were red – no carpet, except on the walls. At least Surinder had the impression that the walls were a fiery orange or a deep purple but it was difficult to tell because everything was so sprinkled over with *things*. Suns and moons and planets and parrots and seagulls and pierrots-on-stars and babies-on-clouds dangled and spun before the eyes all around the stairs area, and in the main room were shawls and feathers and velvet and net and a black lace fan half-closed like a butterfly's wings, cables of sequins and beads, and posters and hanging plants and plaited string and jangling shells and bells. A moose's head with a sparkly necklace round it jutted out of the wall and the room smelt of moth-balls and wood smoke, marmalade, cinnamon and pine. In the middle of the floor was a grand piano. It was painted green where it wasn't all over flowers and ferns and fabulous beasts. There was no other furniture – just large cushions – and

a great many books. No bookcases. They simply spilt
and toppled about.

Topaz told Surinder to sit down and clattered off up the
stairs screeching 'Mum!' The kitchen door opened and a
little girl came out.

She looked like a child from a nursery rhyme with her
blonde hair cut square round her cheeks and her full deep
fringe. She was dressed in an all-in-one striped suit like a
clown's with big red pom-poms down the front. She came
over to Surinder and stood in front of him, staring. At last
she said, 'Why you got a tea-cosy on your head?'

She didn't wait for a reply. 'I'm making up songs about
carrots this week,' she told him. 'Do you want "Carrots
Go on a Picnic" or "Carrots Cleaning Their Teeth"?'

Surinder opened his mouth. There was a colossal
stampeding on the stairs and Topaz's legs appeared, followed by the bottom half of what turned out to be a large
woman in a dragon-covered dressing-gown with a bandage
of plaited scarves around her head.

'Surinder!' she said, holding out her hand. 'Hullo there.
You've met William, I see. Take Surinder into the kitchen,
Topaz, and let him find himself something to eat.'

Surinder was so astonished to discover the clown suit
housed a *boy* that he'd followed Topaz into the kitchen
before he'd had a chance to mumble that he hadn't the time.
Surinder was glad he'd been told beforehand that the room
he'd just entered was the kitchen because everything was
dressed up to look like something else. The cooker looked
like the Space Control Center at Houston, the table was a
toadstool, the stools were mushrooms, and rose-coloured
clouds floated past the window across a clear blue sky,
though Surinder distinctly remembered it had started to
rain. Topaz flung open a fridge door that had been painted

all over with spiders complete with their webs. 'What would you like?' she asked, and Surinder peered in. He swallowed and thought desperately, deciding they couldn't interfere too much with a bottle of milk. What price a tissue box covered with computer paper and labelled TISSUES in bold black ink after *this*?

'Just a glass of milk, please,' said Surinder weakly. Topaz pulled a face but she handed him the bottle and a ruby red plastic drinking mug with a yellow plastic straw snaking out of it. He noticed she poured milk for herself in an *ordinary* glass, but to this she immediately added a dash of blackcurrant juice and stirred it all up with a spoon disguised as a spanner. She carved herself bread from a hefty-looking loaf and piled on a lot of purply pink salami. She held it up against the contents of the glass and nodded. 'I do so like my food to *tone*,' she explained to a mystified Surinder, taking a gulp of the violet-coloured milk.

As Topaz gulped, a multi-hued bird with wings like a feather boa flung itself out of a clock with a Kermit the Frog face and an upside-down rainbow for a mouth. It eeyored twice to mark the half-hour and Surinder's time-table flapped straight out of the rose-tinted window as he beheld Topaz's lilac moustache and the tawny pony-tail springing out of one ear. And his heart jerked and boinged in time to the grand piano which at that moment struck up an improvised tune to 'Carrots Cleaning Their Teeth'. For Surinder Sewing Machine Singh and Topaz Matilda-Jane Smith, time simply stood still.

That night Surinder's father yelled up the stairs to say that they were five, eight, twelve, *fifteen* minutes into 'News at Ten' and Surinder's Relaxing Drink had developed a skin. Surinder, however, was busy explaining to Delroy that he wasn't going to be a brain surgeon after all but would be owning a whole chain of jewellers' shops instead. In each of his stores he would be dedicating an entire window to displaying a single gem and in every one there would be a scroll curling out of a broken alarm clock, emblazoned with the device 'A Topaz is For Ever . . .' His father hollered up the stairs for absolutely the last time to recall to his son's mind the grave importance of keeping up with World Events. But Surinder didn't even hear him as he started his fourth closely packed page to his Birmingham friend . . .